Rhythms of Life

Stories published earlier:
(*in a slightly different form*)

'A Local': in the **Indian Literature**, published by the Sahitya Akademi, India's National Academy of Letters, New Delhi. Volume: 227, May-June 2005.

'Aditi', Indian Literature. Volume:237, Jan-Feb 2007

Editor: Mr.Nirmal Kanti Bhattacharjee.

'Mr. So and So': in the **Creative Edge, The Sunday Pioneer**. New Delhi.

May 2004.

'Visage': in **The 8th Day, The Sunday Statesman Magazine**, Kolkata

December14, 2003.

'Passion': in the **India Perspective** published by the Ministry of External Affairs

(Government of India), New Delhi.

November 2004.

'The Sariwallah':in the **India Perspective** August 2005.

Translated: French, Spanish, Arabic, Urdu, Hindi, Portuguese, Russian, Bahasa Indonesia and German

Editor: Mr. Bharat Bhushan.

Rhythms of Life

Nilakshi Borgohain

B. R. Publishing Corporation
Delhi-110052

Cataloging in Publication Data--DK

Courtesy: D.K. Agencies (P) Ltd. <docinfo@dkagencies.com>

Borgohain, Nilakshi.

Rhythms of life / Nilakshi Borgohain.

p. cm.

Short stories.

ISBN 8176466409

1. Short stories, Indic (English). I. Title.

DDC 823 22

First Published 2008

ISBN 81-7646-640-9

Rs. 145/-

Published by :

B. R. Publishing Corporation

425, Nimri Colony,

Ashok Vihar, Phase-IV

Delhi – 110052

E-Mail : *brpc@vsnl.com*

This is a work of fiction. As in all fiction, the literary perceptions may be based on experience, while all names, characters, and incidents are fictious. Hence no reference to any real person is intended or should be inferred.

Cover photograph : Satya brata Borgohain

Cover design : Neeraj Mittal, New Delhi.

ACKNOWLEDGEMENTS

I started my writing journey as a schoolgirl. So my teachers deserve special mention for steering my interest toward books.

Sincere gratitude goes out to Dr. Indira Raisome Goswami, Jnapith award winner, for constantly encouraging me to continue writing even when the going got real tough. Mr. Bharat Bhushan for being the ideal unbiased editor and publishing my short stories in a magazine of such high standard so spontaneously. Thank you for your confidence in my work. Mr. Nirmal Kanti Bhattacharjee, for your faith in my work and for encouraging me by generously publishing my stories in the Sahitya Academi journals. Mr. A.J.Thomas, Upasana and Sanjay from Sahitya Akademi, New Delhi, deserve particular mention for your gracious cooperation.

To all my dear friends and well wishers whose conversations invariably start with a: 'So when do we get to read your next story?' Pradeep and Deepanjali Sinha, Tripura; Renu Gulati, Manju Consel and Rita Sinha, Sarita Vihar, New Delhi, Dr Brian Mendonca, Goa.Mr. Vishnu Sahai and Anita Bedi, International Cultural Center, Gurgaon;, Mrs. Rumi Sharma, Dwarka, Mr. Bidyut Kumar, Gurgaon, Gundeep and Himat Sekhon, Amritsar; Balaka Agarwallah, New Delhi, Dr. Borthakur, Shillong; Mrs. Ruma Sharma, Shrimati Syeda Anwara Taimur, New Delhi Zareen Ali, Philippines; Mrs.Neeti Koshik, Gurgaon; Prof. Nancy Shabong, Shillong. Bharati Charan, Mumbai. Dambaru Datta, Dr. & Mrs. Khiren Roy, Guwahati.Mr Vijay Dagar, Haryana.A special thank you to Mrs. Pratima Thakuria and Mr. Manuj Das, Assam Association, New Delhi and Mr. Mridul Bhuyan, Mr. Pranjal Goswami and Mr. Gautam Hazarika of the Gurgaon Assamese Association for publishing my stories with such touching eagerness. Thank you all.

All my family members whose love and hope make my appreciation of their presence in my life so much dearer. My parents, Mrs. Indushri and Mr. P.K.Gogoi. My sister and brother-in- law, Meenakshi and Surajit Baruah.

And all the other family members who have always read my work with appreciation. Rondeep Baruah, Guwahati; Col.Ranjit Baruah, Hyderabad; Rupa and Utpal Borsaikia, Leena and Ananda Borgohain, Guwahati; Niva Konwar, New Delhi; Dileep Baruah, Dhubri. Mr. Biren Borgohain, Mrs.Bhanu Gogoi Ms. Nandita Konwar and Mr. Debabrata Borgohain.

A very special thank you to Mr.Praveen Mittal and Mr Niraj Mittal of BR Publications, New Delhi for their support and guidance in publishing 'Rhythms of Life'.

Satya, thank you for everything. Finally, Gautam (Jolly) and Aishwarya-you two are the sunshine of my life!

— *Nilakshi Borgohain*

CONTENTS

THE GARDEN OF ABUNDANCE

Psalm103: 15-16

As for a man, his days are as grass: as a flower of the field, so he flourisheth. For the wind passeth over it, and it is gone; and the place thereof shall know it no more.

Pallavi paced around agitatedly in her brand new home. If one could call it home. A sense of claustrophobia suffocated her. From a life thus far spent in beautiful bungalows with luxurious lawns and expansive gardens, her romantic flight suffered a temporary setback when she discovered that all Rahul could afford was a two bedroom apartment in an underdeveloped locality in the suburbs of the capital city.

Her lifestyle as the daughter of one of the celebrated personalities in town included a travesty of literary and cultural interactions along with an attempt at social service in the manner of teaching children with special needs in the school founded by her mother. All her activities, however, came to a standstill once she relocated. She lived barely twenty miles away from the capital's City Center, yet all her outings were restricted to her husband's ability to accompany her. There was no public transport available around for two miles and walking was out of question as the road that led from her house towards the nearest bus stop six kilometers away had more dusty craters than a smooth patch of earth. A blacktopped road appeared a distant dream.

Once, she valiantly trekked down the road up to the bus stop and took a bus to enjoy a ballet performance in the capital. But the trip physically exhausted her rather than in any way mentally rejuvenate her. Frustrated, she decided to abandon her city life. Her conversations with her parents and friends dwindled over the days and weeks that passed by. Her landline was unreliable and the signal in her cell phone was accessible exclusively in her front balcony. The strain of speaking in stage whispers to make herself audible to the caller and inaudible to the continuous flow of labours loitering below their apartment took its toll on her telephonic conversations as well. The effort wore out her penchant of passing time chatting with her friends.

Finding herself thus trapped inside her flat, she pranced around within its walls like a restless young lioness locked up in a cage .The neighbourhood was inhabited by middle class folks who had moved from the capital as well as from the neighbouring states. None of the women could honestly afford to while away a couple of hours a day nibbling biscuits over cups of tea.

They kept busy pursuing teaching jobs in the numerous schools that had sprung in the vicinity to cater to the needs of the burgeoning new floating population. Or by chasing a career in the Call Centers that had mushroomed all around the city. Every family appeared to have taken a loan to purchase a new home and a swanky car to upgrade their lifestyle. And the husband and wife team worked at furious speed to repay their loans. The women woke up at the crack of dawn to prepare *chapattis* (Indian bread) and *subzi* (fried vegetables) for their children's, husbands' as well as for their own lunchboxes. Those who could afford a fulltime maid to take care of their little tots were spared this drudgery for the maids helped with the cooking as well. Then, depending on their place of work, they dashed off to their schools in the school vans or ran to jump up at the honking jeeps from the Call Centers. Life for them was a mad rush in pursuit of fulfilling all their material desires. Their weekends were meticulously time tabled with visits to their-in-laws, relatives and the countless pending household chores, which invariably piled up during the hectic week.

Pallavi, with the arrogance of youth, had disdainfully scorned the possessions her mother so proudly displayed. Her marriage to Rahul was her decisive gesture of defiance against her parents. Her mother had fretted and fumed and raised a dozen objections. And when all her pleadings and threats failed, she gifted her daughter a cottage near her home, and a car for Pallavi to drive around independently. Pallavi, bent upon seeking her own brand of happiness in the arms of nature, declined to accept her mother's presents.

So why was she mourning over her self imposed confinement away from the excessive baggage of the consumerist society? As she stood in her sizable front balcony, brooding upon the barren landscape, a hawker passed by announcing his wares in a sing song voice, 'Earthen flower pots and seasonal flower plants for sale. The best your money can buy.'

Pallavi brought a dozen pots and an equal number of plants. As she resided in the second floor, she purchased two sacks full of manure and soil. She even asked the seller to bring five more 5 feet by2feet cement tubs. With the warm early winter sunshine wrapping her body like a soft cocoon, she spent the entire day planting. As she surveyed her handiwork by the fading light of the swift approach of early dusk, the colours of all those flowers brought a smile to her lips. The mingling of fragrances of the yellow marigolds, purple petunias, azure asters, sapphire sweetwilliams, crimson carnations and white jasmines pleasantly elevated her spirits. For the very first time since she had shifted to her new home two months earlier, she pulled a chair out to the balcony and sipped her evening tea in her brand new little garden. Her husband found her still sitting at the same spot when he returned home from office. She greeted him with a wide smile, asking him to freshen up while she prepared tea. They sat drinking tea, munching cup cakes and talking until the moon and the stars made their appearance in the wide expanse of the sky above them. Always having lived in cities, they were both enthralled by the sight of a clear pollution free sky.

The next day, the hawker brought the tubs Pallavi had asked for. She purchased several bougainvillea cuttings and *champa* plants this time along with a few bulbs of brightly blooming lavender, orange and white dahlias. She arranged the tubs with the help of the seller on either side of the wide ledges of the front and back balconies. The fifth tub, she set in the middle of the ledge of her kitchen balcony. In the back balcony, which received plenty of afternoon sunshine, she planted roses. She chose climbing roses to decorate the two pillars on either side of the balcony. She concentrated on bedding roses for enhancing the ornamentation of her rose garden because they had a long period of bloom. There were countless varieties of roses-the Asian damask rose, the French rose, the double cabbage rose of the Caucasus, the China rose and the tea rose. Whenever they left the tiny window of their bedroom open, a seductively heady perfume wafted indoors.

The kitchen garden developed a character of its own as Pallavi habitually planted the seeds of the lemons, oranges, papayas, mangoes she used for her cooking .A four feet hardy papaya tree nurtured deliciously sweet fruits-the size of alphonso mangoes. The diminutive mango tree provided richly aromatic leaves for performing her *pujas* (religious ceremonies). The onion bulbs she planted ensured a regular supply of fresh spring onions to dress up omelets. Coriander, parsley, mint, basil and neem leaves took care of her herbal needs in the kitchen. And when the first lemon made its appearance in all its emerald green glory and a deliciously heady tangy flavour, it became the prime topic of their ritual teatime conversation.

The front balcony garden symbolized the most idyllic vision of all of life's hues and fullness. The temple trees might have grown in their miniature version within the restricted space but their lustrous white flowers with their luminous golden centers were heavily scented, enticing the evening breeze to linger even into the sultry summer nights. Evergreens included miniatures of pines, willows and silver oaks. They provided the background for the shrubs and seasonal flowers. The inconspicuous bougainvillea flowers each flaunted their three large showy bracts in their riotous colours of outrageous pinks, virgin white and shocking scarlet, resembling delicately coloured snowflakes in their thorny bushes. The flamboyant Gulmohar tree, she trained flat against the wall and tied its stylish branches there to give it a two dimensional effect. Her own version of espalier gardening, which the French would definitely be able to find a word of praise were they ever to lay their eyes on this unique wall tree.

The pot of white jasmine was far more sensuously sweet smelling than the most exquisite French perfume. In such a profusion of colour and fragrance, it took little time for birds and butterflies of a myriad species to visit Pallavi's garden transforming her decorative garden into a vibrant paradise. Overwhelmed by the songs of the birds, Pallavi purchased a shallow wide rimmed terracotta bowl to use it as a birdbath. She filled the bowl with fresh water every morning and placed it on the milky white marbled ledge in the front balcony near the hibiscus plant. In due course of time a branch curved itself around the basin almost encircling its rim with its tender green leaves.

Soon, pigeons, doves, mynas, sparrows, bulbuls, sunbirds, babblers, minivets, flycatchers, starlings, parakeets and robins regularly visited their miniature pond for a sip and perhaps even a dip. The babblers created enough ruckus around it to give it the feel of a village well where the village women gossiped animatedly as they filled their water pots. While the doves and all the other so called wild birds drank and soaked themselves nonchalantly in Pallavi's presence, the well endowed pigeons, considered extremely domestic due to their persistence in inhabiting within human territory, always clumsily tripped and splashed the water in their rush to engineer a swift exit. Until Pallavi arranged a home for them by securing a two feet by one feet light wooden box below the ledge in the right corner of the balcony. She carefully lined the box with plastic before making it a comfortable habitat with the dry pine needles from her miniature pine trees in her garden. Presently, the entire family of pigeons not only drank their full but also ate tiny bowlful of grains Pallavi placed near the water bowl.

The thick green background foliage with the array of shrubs and seasonal flowers cushioned them from the noise of the never-ending sea of humanity that appeared to be the hallmark of every middleclass colony. The sounds of the wailing children neglected by the maids, the incessant honking of impatient drivers, the horribly frustrating barking of huge pet dogs shut inside small houses without an opportunity to get enough exercise... Initially, it appeared to Pallavi that only the super rich were able to afford to live in isolated splendour in their palatial residences and clean lanes lined with verdant *neem* and *jamun* trees. Pallavi's little garden provided ample protection against the dust constantly stirred up by the seemingly unending construction activities.

The garden presented a comfortable setting, which induced Rahul and Pallavi to open their hearts to discover each other. Rahul related an amusing incident, which he had mentally registered to share with Pallavi that evening.

"This morning, the entire department was stinking of over ripe guavas. You know, that stale odour I absolutely abhor. I poked around the other executives' cubicles to check whether the sweepers had left behind some unclean dustbins. I had visions of the fruit rotting to a black pulpy lump, lying somewhere within the confines of our department .The stink was so offensively foul. After a futile investigation as I sat clueless to the origin of the smell, the Big Cheese buzzed for me. Soon as I entered his chamber, all my senses were assaulted by the stench of a zillion rotten guavas. There, in the Boss's chamber, lay the origin of my discomfort- a mountainful of overripe guavas elaborately arranged in a dish on his desk. Chomping at the fruit he gleefully explained that he had taken to feasting entirely on guavas twice a week. His guru had enlightened him on the multifarious goodness of the great fruit. As he declared his intention I knew I had to dissuade him from his mission if I wished to survive in the office. With as grave an expression I could muster, I advised him that it is best to go easy on fruits like guavas and restrict their intake to breakfast. I recounted in detail the dreadful effect it had on my uncle DhaniKanta who died due to the growth of a huge stone in his stomach, which the doctors diagnosed, was caused by the intake of guava seeds. Uncle DhaniKanta had an orchard of guava trees and he had been a voracious guava eater. I barely completed my tale before Big Boss pushed aside his fruit dish, wiped his mouth with a paper napkin and declared he had eaten enough guavas."

"How come I have never heard anyone in the family mention your uncle DhaniKanta?"Pallavi asked incredulously.

"Because he never existed. Just a spur of the moment character I invented to foil Big Man's attempt at turning the office into a guava chamber."Rahul grinned.

Pallavi laughed. She could laugh, Rahul mused. She laughed shaking her hands and feet wildly and continued laughing until tears rolled down her cheeks and she almost started choking as she doubled up her body to control her bout of merriment.

It soon became a ritual. Every evening, Rahul looked forward to their conversations in their garden. Any interesting incident that transpired during the course of the day, he would religiously share with Pallavi. The garden with its ambiance of abundance indulged them to talk, to laugh, to relax. The serenity surrounding it induced them to share their deepest secrets, darkest fears and greatest ambitions. The garden literally sought to portray the oneness of their relationship. As she planted each new sapling she knew Rahul would derive as much pleasure from the blossoming of the flowers as she would. She began to spend much of her free time tending the garden. Overwhelmed by the result of her labour of love, she began experimenting successfully with delicate temperate glories like the narcissus and the tulip.

She installed a small terracotta fountain and eventually, they had the sparkling resonance of water sublimate the meditative silences during their conversations.

One such evening, Rahul suggested they invite their friends over for dinner .It was nearly two years since they had moved and they had not once hosted a party at their home. Rahul decided it would be a good idea to include a couple of his office colleagues as well.

On the night of the party, to add a festive glitter, Pallavi filled lavishly aromatic candles snugly in plump round *diyas* (earthen lamps) and placed them strategically underneath the shrubs and bushes that gave the garden a romantically ethereal appearance. Tarun, Rahul's best friend, declared gallantly that Rahul was the luckiest man to have found a treasure like Pallavi.

"Pallavi epitomizes Thalia, the *blossoming one.* One of the Graces symbolizing beauty and charm of young women." He elaborated.

"Why compare her to a Greek mythological character,"challanged Rana. "Her name itself means *tender leaves.* No wonder she's got green fingers!"

The Public Relations officer Tina glowered with resentment. As the only woman in her forties (and claiming to be still in her thirties), she was used to the other executives' undivided attention at the office. Their courtesy being diverted from her to Pallavi for an entire evening proved too irksome for her to tolerate. None of the other wives had appeared a greater threat to her undisputed aptitude to thus arrest everyone's interest. Pallavi certainly seemed poised to jeopardize the situation. During the course of that very first meeting, Tina decided that it would be extremely easy to dislike Pallavi.She realized she needed to act quickly and annihilate the bud at its nib, to avoid Pallavi usurp her painstakingly maintained seat of superiority.

Tina swooped into action just as everyone was busy thanking and praising Pallavi for a wonderful evening. She gently whispered into Rahul's ears how Pallavi looked so utterly innocent but was so totally selfishly taking all the praise on maintaining an enchanting garden instead of acknowledging Rahul's contribution in it. Tina's soft words reverberated in Rahul's mind. He forgot it was he who had promised Pallavi that they would mutually take pride in each other's success . His tranquil mind distorted into a whirlwind of redness. As the last guest drove away, he huffed up the staircase, two steps at a time and broke the fountain in the garden with a hard kick into small pieces.

Pallavi stared at the fragmented bits of terracotta scattered in careless disharmony. A word, an action, a fraction of a second was all it took to destroy a symbolism of love, of life, of hope. The banging of the bedroom door momentarily indicated the presence of life in the flat that was suddenly enveloped in an eerie silence.

Pallavi sat down wearily on a garden chair. Overwhelmed by a feeling of being struck by the muse of tragedy, Melpomene. She definitely needed time to blow away the cobwebs.

Kamikaze, some divine wind must have swept across the garden. The capacity of the garden to harmonize and heal her senses no matter how bad she felt was tremendous. The fountain could be replaced. But Rahul would need a little more time to help him realize the pettiness of selfishness in a relationship. Methodically, she started trimming stems of roses, tulips, petunias, daisies and asters. She arranged them in a beautiful bouquet and sent them across to Tina the next morning with a short note thanking her for her gracious presence at the dinner.

Tina looked at the abundance of natural colours of the fragrant blossoms delivered to her. Her essential empathy, which she had sold off to the Mephistopheles of greed and ambition, burst from its power-driven constraints and she was shocked to witness tears flood her smooth powdered cheeks. She felt like a stranger observing her body struggle with long suppressed emotions.

Pallavi, who had only hoped for a faint ray of positivism from Tina was amazed by the miracle her flowers evoked. Marveling how those blossoms tenderly nudged Tina into apologizing to Rahul of trying to cause trouble in his marriage. Tina went so far as to admire Pallavi's nature.

'So unsoiled by this jaded world. She brings to my mind the words of the great King Ashoka,the ruthlessly ambitious King who was reformed by the words of a Buddhist *bhikshu* after the bloody battle of Kalinga.Ashoka had asserted that: without self control, purity of thought, gratitude and firm devotion, a person is quite worthless... these words ring so true of her.' Tina said.

That evening, as Rahul sat with Pallavi in their garden and watched the sun set in a spectacular orange ball of fire, he realized the garden not only brought them bliss, it also helped them spread and share joy. The garden added that divine dimension to their lives; it taught them to forgive.

A Local

Aparajita Phukan vigorously wiped her eyes of the remainder of recurring drowsiness with her frail fists. It was her Grandfather's roaring voice that nudged awoke her sleep-induced senses. She swiftly jumped out of the comfort of her warm bed laden with quilts stuffed with the softest cotton from the Garo Hills. The quilts were fluffed annually just before the onset of winters by the *dhunnawallas* who came from Katihar in Bihar. They blew the rich quality cotton in a cloud of cumulus with their bowstrings and the old quilts again became soft as dawn to cuddle snugly in the cold moist nights. She ran to the bathroom to brush her teeth and swiftly changed from her nightdress into a warm pair of slacks and a cashmere pullover. She skipped out into the compound where her grandfather awaited her. His dark craggy face flowered into a smile transforming his habitually severe countenance with joie de vivre at the sight of the little girl.

He picked his ivory walking stick and they set out on their morning walk. They made an interesting subject-the grandfather and his little grandchild. Grandfather always wore his black overcoat during the foggy winter mornings. This added extra bulk to his already large frame. The child walking beside him looked as fragile as a blushing poppy in bloom. While the grandfather's heavy stride appeared to leave imprints of his footsteps on the ground he treaded upon, the child's ballerina-like steps barely touched the ground to bestow a light kiss upon it. The cold stained the child's rich creamy cheeks like a shade of crimson on the thick velvety petals of a buttery rose.

For all their physical disparities, they were in perfect mental harmony with each other. They inhaled with immense satisfaction the fresh mist laden air, fragrant with the aroma of tealeaves. They simultaneously exclaimed with rapture at the sight of the snow-white cranes resting on their cinnamon hued pencil thin feet upon the luxuriantly green tea shrubs. The tall trees planted to protect the tender tealeaves towered over them presenting a view of superabundance of nature as well as a spectacular visual delight.

Their walk was never complete without the Grandfather recounting some anecdote or the other of his childhood. They would return home after an hour to be greeted by the warmth of Grandmother's smile and a delicious and hearty breakfast.

Aparajita enjoyed her annual fortnightly sojourn at her Grandparent's house in Dibrugarh.The remaining days of her three-month long winter vacation would be spent with her parents in their sprawling tea garden estate with a short visit to a new place within the country or out of it. Like most of the children of the tea garden executives, she studied in a boarding school in Shillong.It was a convent school where they were taught by the nuns who mostly were from countries like England, Ireland and Australia. They bequeathed to their pupils a sense of responsibility, underlining the importance of accountability for every action. Her parents visited her every month. And then there were the short summer and autumn breaks as well when she either came home or the entire family went on a holiday.

At home it was Tulsi, her personal maid who was her best friend. Tulsi's father's parents had migrated from Bihar and worked as tea garden labourers. Her mother was from Orissa.She worked in the kitchen. It was only when Aparajita came home that Tulsi volunteered to work in the Phukan household. Tulsi was almost as dark as the *kajal* that she adorned her exquisite large eyes with. When Aparajita came home, Tulsi would refuse to attend school and spend as much time as possible with Aparajita.Aparajita helped her perfect her English and Assamese. The two girls spent their time trekking unexplored terrain, playing lawn tennis and participating in the *jhumur* dance of the tea garden community. On turning a teenager Aparajita began accompanying her parents to the Dances at the Club. She would adamantly insist upon Tulsi accompanying them as well. Both the girls had a natural rhythm. Whether it was the Punjabi *bhangra*, the Gujarati *dandiya*, the *jhumur* or the Assamese *bihu* dance-their grace lent that unique elegance to the dance.

On 26th January, the Republic Day, Aparajita's mother would ritually unlock an old trunk that was religiously painted at regular intervals to a shiny black exterior finish and red as a lusciously ripe tomato in the inside. With the greatest care she would cradle out the silk tricolour, that lay snugly wrapped in a soft muslin material.

Aparajita's father would unfurl the flag with immense national pride. The flag would blow gently in the wind the entire day- high on its aluminum pole atop the round-cemented platform, freshly painted in white amidst the baby green grass. After a special tea, which was an elaborate affair of freshly baked cakes and piping hot, fried to a golden perfection small round balls of salted *pitas* cooked with rice flour and finely chopped seasonal vegetables, it was time to unfurl the flag .It was then pressed and folded and replaced in the trunk with fresh mothballs.

Time in its eternal restlessness soon transported the girls into the realm of adulthood, poised for an independent insight into the complexities of life. Aparajita went to the country's capital to pursue a graduation degree in one of the reputed colleges. Tulsi joined the local college fifteen kilometers away from the tea garden. Aparajita, who had secured an excellent percentage in the school leaving board examinations, let her Grandfather decide on the college of his choice for her. It was her Grandfather who had overridden her mother's objection of Aparajita going to Delhi for studies by reminding her how she had gone out to Beneras to pursue her studies decades back. Reminding her how he himself had traveled to England for further studies. He reiterated the importance of learning through interaction to achieve a well-rounded education.

Once at the hostel, it took Aparajita a while to comprehend that her identity as an Indian would always need an explanation. It was no longer a fundamental truth to be indisputably accepted. Everywhere she went, everyone she spoke to, she was questioned and asked to elaborate exactly of which area she was a local. Initially it felt bizarre to be constantly answering questions on her origins and her raison d'être on being there. Why had she opted for Delhi University? (Wasn't education much more than just books?) Weren't there any good colleges in the region she came from? (Wasn't it the best way to learn more about a culture by being a part of it for any period of time?) Didn't she miss the lovely hills of home? (That's where she spent her holidays didn't she?) How long were her plans to stay on in Delhi after completion of her studies? (Had any of them really thought of so far ahead?) Strange. None of the students had ever asked one another any awkward questions on the subject of one's region of origin except, perhaps as a topic of passing interest, during her years in school. The cosmopolitan outlook had been far more pronounced in that small hill station.

But an apparently insignificant incident in itself would almost on a regular basis raise within her the ugly question on the correctness in her decision in opting to reside for all practical purpose in a place other than that of one's own locality.

Like it happened one day while she was with a friend of hers at a restaurant, the waiter came over to ask her preference for the brand of bottled water mentioning they even stocked Evian. When she requested for the regular pure drinking water they were supposed to supply free of charge to the customers, the waiter confidentially told her that drinking water in Indian restaurants was always a perilous proposition. She informed him precisely from which part of the country she was from. To which he responded that she avoid spending unnecessarily on mineral water at all! The water in the region she came from was far more contaminated anyway he spoke sagely.

Aparajita's un-Indian appearance landed her in unusual situations. She belonged to the Thai Ahom race that had ruled Assam for a period of six hundred years. Her ancestors had migrated across the Patkai hills into Assam in1228AD. Like most Indians; the Thai Ahoms were not the original inhabitants of India. But their 600 years rule had been architecturally, socio-culturally, politically and economically a stupendously glorious period. They had successfully resisted even the Mogul invasion seventeen times. Finally it was Raja Purandar Singha's inability to repay the tribute that he had been bound to pay the 'Honourable Company' that Assam became a part of British territory and the royal families were pensioned off.

Visiting public places and attending functions became an ordeal as her features signaled her out for extra scrutiny and security check. She wryly tried to contemplate what a complex confusion their formative years in school would have resulted in had they looked upon everyone from beyond the Vindyas as the nefarious dacoit, Verrapan's relations. Certainly, none of the people from all the diverse nooks of the country who had settled there were looked upon with askance on entering any store in the manner of a robber who had sauntered in minus the mask and the gun, but with the definitive intention of robbing nonetheless. Sadly, she did belong to what had become a backward zone of a third world country .So what if Assam had actually regressed as India had progressed? From being the land of great hope with its abundance in tea, oil, coal and teak and a GDP higher than the national average till the Planning process began in the country, it had now sunk to the lowest positions.

'Fresher, you don't smoke. You don't drink. You don't do drugs. You don't even have a boyfriend. And your nose is always buried in a book. How can you claim to be from the North East?' A senior, carrying forward the age-old practice of ragging a fresher, had drawled in a heavily affected American accent. Aparajita had maliciously wondered whether the senior was deluded by the impression that all the North Americans were still cowboys, riding horses *a la* Clint Eastwood style, shooting down the bad guys at the slightest provocation.

Blanketing humans of any region under any particular identity can always prove to be a dangerous hypothesis .Of course, the level of literacy and advancement varying from time to time play a major role in molding the thoughts and ideas of any particular community inhabiting any specific place on earth. Strictly speaking, it wasn't the senior's fault. Really. She recalled her maiden trip to Mumbai as a six year old when she had insisted upon visiting the red light area thinking it was the locale where the young men and women danced around in the gardens like they showed in the Hindi movies. She had come across the colorful phrase in the newspapers. That had been the precise elucidation her Grandmother had wriggled out giving of the meaning of a red light area when Aparajita had pestered her with an explanation of the meaning of the term. Now of course, her cheeks grew hot in embarrassment when she recollected her parents' stunned expressions at her extraordinary request.

After graduation, her marriage to an executive working in a multinational company bought her to Gurgaon where the question of originality assumed wackier proportions. 'Where on earth was Shillong?' 'Didn't she mean Ceylon?' 'Was Assam a part of India?' 'Did she know magic?'(People of the region practiced witchcraft, didn't they?) Weren't the men from the north east violent, insurgent head hunters and man-eaters?'(Ouch!). These questions baffled her for they came from the most unlikely source-the educated literate class. She mused what their response would be if she asked them questions on how many of them had had child marriages, how many of them would be joining their husbands in their funeral pyres as *sati*, how many of them would be sacrificing their girl child to relieve themselves of the burden of dowry harassment? Education, modernization and awareness had been successfully eroding such narrow-minded superstitious practices amongst the people through the ages much in the manner of new molten lava spreading in a golden sea of change over all the grime collected through the ages. Who could blame the poor educated lot for never having heard of Assam? The history books in their school days had almost always been totally silent of such a land for a long time. It was AIDS, drugs, insurgency and associated titillating reports with an extra zest of exotic strangeness that generally made it to the news. The charm of the region had been marred like a newly wedded beautiful bride upon whom life had tainted all its harsh blemishes on her countenance for she had neglected to take care of her self. This was partially due to a sense of self-complacency and partly due to lack of an opportunity.

Was it any wonder that the Chief Engineer from South India with his riotously curly, black, sleekly coconut oiled hair, whom they had once met at the club had grandly announced that he had come down to offer them solace from the annual floods by constructing the biggest dam in the region? Aparajita's father had reminded him in jest that the sole reason for his being there was because he had been posted to the region. The colonial attitude of the Chief Engineer was unfortunate for he was in other respects a likeable fellow and could play a good game of tennis. However, he soon made an effort to understand and appreciate the opulence of the region and it was almost with a sense of sorrow they bade him farewell when he was transferred.

It was a few weeks after Aparajita had moved to Gurgaon, and was busy preparing dinner for a few friends she had invited over, that Rajlakshmi her neighbour, walked into the kitchen to borrow some curd. Rajlakshmi's eyes fell upon the slices of firm *hilsa* fish coated in *haldi* and salt. She let out an involuntary scream at the sight. Aparajita, looking at the plateful of delicacy through Rajlakshmi's eyes understood her instinctive repugnance although poor Rajlakshmi tried to mask her aversion as swiftly, as best as she could. Nervously flapping her hands as she grappled to explain how it was the very first time she had seen raw non-vegetarian food being prepared for cooking purpose. She even managed a smile and rolled her eyes heavenward in a gesture of self-mockery. Aparajita felt a new admiration for Rajlakshmi.But it was a long time before she could bring herself to eat and relish fish with equal gusto. The knowledge that fish was an essential item of delicacy in Assam, that it was considered auspicious enough to be a part of the *joron* the groom's family presented the bride with prior to the marriage ceremony as a symbol of longevity and prosperity, did nothing to assuage her sense of guilt every time she held a spoonful of fish to eat. Rajlakshmi's expression plagued her mind, disturbed her soul.

Gurgaon was an old town whose outskirts were invaded by the urban dwellers coming in hordes to settle down in this suburb near Delhi. For Aparajita it was always an enlightening experience to meet new people from the various states of the country. However, she found it easier pretending to be a foreigner in public places. It saved her the unnecessary harassment of having to explain her historical roots, geographical location, economical position and of course the omnipresent question about the political scenario in the areas. The volley of questions ranged from the silly to the downright absurd. Is Assam a jungle? Is monogamy practiced there? (Why? Had the Government of India passed a new legislation legalizing bigamy?) To curtail such nonsensical questions it was easier to pretend to be from some far eastern country. Furthermore, it elicited more respect and better service. She refused to suffer from any qualms of guilt on these trivial lies she lisped out on her origin to cut short any unnecessary conversation and preserve a wee bit of her privacy. The questions written in the faces of the strangers were ever present. Mere eye contact would pave the path for the question boiling to erupt: 'Where are you from?'

While visiting a fair in Delhi's Pragati Maidan with two of her friends from Meerut and Lucknow, she was signaled out and thoroughly frisked by the security woman asking her to empty all the contents of her purse. She finally completed the humiliation by remarking that she had seen Aparajita visit the same pavilion earlier in the day. Unfortunately, Aparajita, with her sheltered upbringing was in no position to argue the validity of the questioner's insinuation. Strictly speaking, the lady was after all only performing her duty, even though, it was equally true that she could have performed her duty with a little more fineness and not made her personal apprehension on folks of a particular region quite so evident. Frazzled at being thus questioned, Aparajita mumbled nervously an incoherent response. Anita, her friend, intervened to challenge the security officer on the implication of such a leading question. Aparajita swiftly steered Anita out of the spot to avoid any unnecessary unpleasantness. Anita fumed, Aparajita's ears burnt red and Atifa tried to ease the tension by introducing a new topic in their conversation to salvage some enjoyment out of their outing.

This unsavoury incident troubled Aparajita for days. It took her husband several weeks to succeed in persuading her out to dinner. She was developing a strong apathy towards meeting any strangers from around the area. The restaurant her husband chose was a new one. Its owner was an ex-army personnel. When they sat down to start their meal, the owner himself stepped forward to wish them a pleasant evening. Then there was the inevitable pause as his eyes dwelled upon Aparajita.She saw the question hopelessly pregnant around his lips, hovering in his eyes.

'Are you from…?' She patiently waited for him to complete his unfinished sentence. 'Assam?'

Aparajita's jaws gapped open. It was the very first time anyone from the country had made such an accurate assessment. She was vastly overwhelmed. She looked up at him in respect and with a smile full of hope and wonder, responded: 'Yes!'

Mr. So and So

It's not the big things you do that make you great every time. It's that small deed that involuntarily slips away to reveal your true self, which linger on for generations.

He was no longer an extremely important person in the town but many still knew him. A respected gentleman generally held in awe by the people of the town.

He was a wealthy man of great social standing and immense intellectual caliber. He lived in a sprawling white bungalow in a private estate that even boasted of an orchard of citrus fruits. He dwelt there with his wife. He had three daughters and two sons. His wife was a social worker. His sons were corporate lawyers who established a leading firm in the capital city and enhanced their father's fame by building a reputation as the finest in their chosen field of work. His elder daughters' were gynecologists who jointly owned the most reputable Nursing Home in the town.

In such a family of ambitious, hardworking, industrious individuals who grew like healthy flowers with no flaw to point a finger at any member, it would be impossible to dig any grime out of such a beautiful garden had it not been for a minor incident. It was the tiniest of speck that besmirched the pure white sheet of the gentleman's life and career. Nonetheless, it was a defect. A failing that armed people to point a finger at his otherwise unsoiled personality. It somehow pulled him down the few notches necessary to the level of common folks, although perhaps strictly speaking it was not a personal shortcoming on his part. But ordinary mortals like you and me like to believe with desperate self-deception that the anointed are really no different from us and that were it not for the privilege they enjoyed by birth they would be roaming the streets just like us preoccupied with mundane matters that is the hallmark of a middleclass existence.

It was the mystery, which surrounded the case that enlarged the tale into epic proportions. The little speck I had mentioned earlier bloated as if by the splashing of the torrential rains by the gossip mongers' anecdotes and threatened to encompass almost the entire white sheet that had glowed so crystal clear.

The gentleman whose head had always been held high started experiencing trouble trying to ignore the sly glances and mocking smiles when he visited the town to fulfill his social obligations. His head would thunder and rumble and like the flaming orange molten lava in an active volcano, an immense eruption would overcome his body shaking his entire being. Years of self-discipline fortunately enabled him to maintain an impassive facade and greet the general public with his natural affable charm. With each fleeting day it became second nature for him to wear a constant mask to cushion the sporadic hurtful remark. It's surely one of the most amazing traits of humanity how a scandal dies even more slowly than death itself.

The men of the town gloated with satisfaction at being in a position whereby they could pity such a revered gentleman. They smugly discussed with their wives, in the secure confines of their bedroom at night, the relief at not having to face a similar tragedy. No wealth was worth such mental trauma they sagaciously expressed their enlightened view. The complacent wives released a tiny sigh of gratification and agreed, thanking their lot and offering aloud a little prayer.

It was almost a traditon every year that for a week in the summers, all his family members would come and visit him. His sons and daughters would descend upon the family estate with their families and it would be a time for him to take pleasure in the company of his children and grandchildren. His wife would organize a party and invite all their friends and relatives. A carnival like atmosphere prevailed in the festivities that were celebrated in the vast expanse of the manicured lawns. There would be an abundance of laughter, rejoicing, and merrymaking climaxing almost to a pitch of hysterical cacophony. They celebrated all the festivals together. In short, they enjoyed all the pleasures money could buy as one big, happy family.

Each member of his family looked brilliant and cultured. They had the appearance of the rich, well fed and luxuriantly soft. Their demeanor led one to imagine that they surely must have learned their manners and all the principles of etiquette along with their alphabets. They were a close knit family and always stood by each other. This made them powerful, insulating them against mischievous spirits who journey through life with the sole purpose of relishing other people's misfortune.

That tiny speck which he had so far ignored had not bothered him in years. It was only since his eighty-first birthday peoples' opinions began disconcerting him. He had led a complete life, an honest life. He was born to wealth, was educated in the best educational institutions, had held most distinguished official positions and achieved what was of omnipotent importance to him specifically, a respectable social standing in life.

Of late, death had time and again started haunting him in his nightmares. He could almost feel his end approaching with strident footsteps. During such moments he would feel even more powerfully the rage reverberating in his mind. He would break into a sweat as his whole body trembled with the explosive force of darkness that invaded his being. Eventually, the trembling would subside but the turmoil in his mind lasted longer, much longer.

She was his little girl who had touched his practical heart with her baby pink palms and rejuvenated the innocent feelings of love and joy in him. Her gurgling laughter filled him with rapture. She grew up to be the most striking and intelligent in the family making him the proudest father alive. Every time he looked at her, spoke about her, it was apparent to all that he loved her above everyone else in the family. By merely being herself, she emerged to rise above all his achievements and riches to make him feel most triumphant of the fact that he was her father. The laughter the two shared was alluringly bereft of any tinge of pain, any discord of superficiality. The joy one experienced watching such a pure bond filled one with a sense of divine wonder.

Suddenly, one day, in the spring of her youth, the girl ran away from home to marry a boy from a village, a rustic youth whom the family would never stoop to acknowledge as a kin. His appearance was too wild and rugged; his mannerism was loud and boisterous, his social standing nonexistent.

It was truly a blessing for all members of the family except the father that the girl should fall in love with someone so unsuitable. It proved an excellent opportunity to wedge a barrier in the closeness the father and daughter shared. The wily members of the large family wasted no time in cementing the wall of misunderstanding between the two until it stood tall as the Great Wall of China and became sturdier with age due to their constant poisoning of his ears with a nasty yarn too many, of his cherished daughter.

A time soon came when he chose to forget to allow an ephemeral memory of her even during her birthdays. If in some hidden corner of his heart her love and laughter lingered, it was too securely locked away and his numerous commitments and constant demand for attention from the rest of his clan ensured that it was quite redundant to waste precious time over dead matters of the heart. She had run away from home at the ripe old age of eighteen, that was the year he had turned sixty. Somehow, the distance that separated them widened every year and a time even came when her very existence was erased from the minds of the members of the family. Her name was never mentioned by anyone anymore in any context whatsoever. It was as if the eighteen years she was born and nurtured in the household had merely been an illusion.

Being a distinguished gentleman of great social status he could not bend so low as to acknowledge the wife of a man of no patrician pretension, in his will. This brought comfort to all his kith and kin amongst whom he generously divided his assets when he announced the contents of his will on his eighty-second birthday.

That night, after a lavish celebration of his birthday he retired to bed early. It must have been in that period when dawn was languidly descending upon the lingering darkness that he dreamt seeing his little girl in her village home, her hair uncombed, her hands coarse and calloused with hard labour, her face sunburnt with hours of work in the sun, dressed in a cotton attire with no ornaments to enhance her femininity except the pools of merriment that were her eyes which shone like polished diamonds deep in the obscurity of some forgotten mines.

He reached out his hand, trying to gently wipe away the premature lines caused by hunger, worry, pain that etched her bony face. He wanted to soothe her rough windblown hair that had once been so sweetly fragrant and soft. But her image stretched beyond his touch every time he felt he was approaching closer to her. His breathing demanded a valiant effort and he found it increasingly difficult to exert himself for another breath of life .The tender stroke of his little girl gently closing his eyes and ushering him into a splendid vision where the two of them laughed and ran in the green grass towards the brilliantly bright summer sun comforted his weary body battered with the battle of life, his dejected soul.

When the members of the family came to look up on him in the morning, they observed that they were indeed blessed because they had managed to look after him so well. He died a happy man they said. His eyes were closed and the facial muscles around his mouth were tugged into a smile of contentment.

Aditi

This is my story. So you will be stumbling upon the narcissistic pronoun 'I' inordinately repetitively as you strain your intelligence along the text of this tale. My name is Aditi.If I revealed my surname, your mind would conjure a caste, creed, religion and a local to my name and the emotions I wish to deliberate upon in this narrative will be lost in such academic speculation. So let my first name suffice as introduction. That way, no matter which part of the world you are from, you can identify with the woman in this story with the woman within you.

Aditi is a Hindu name. But my father taught me to embrace all the good in all the religions of the world. My faith in God is beyond religious restrictions. My father said Max Muller's interpretation of my name is, 'the visible infinite, visible by the naked eye, the endless expanse beyond the earth, beyond the clouds, beyond the sky'. To my adoring father, I am infinity.

Father taught me to explore the wonder of the world in the ecstatic creation of the Supreme Being -in the colourful blossoming of the striking fuchsia, the brilliant spikes of gladiolus, white, purple stars that flowered in our garden as asters, the flesh coloured carnation, the golden chrysanthemum, the flaming phlox and the stylish and scarlet salvia.

However, a young daughter is always a cause for bittersweet happiness for the parent(s)-if the offspring is blessed with both the parents living. Being without a wife made him an even more conscientious parent. So with all the good intentions throbbing in my father's heart, I was married off with great fanfare at the ripe old age of seventeen. A constitutionally illegal chronological age to wed. But having devoured voluminous volumes curled up on the sofa in my father's study, I was a much-learned seventeen- year -old. Far mature than required of a feme covert.

'She will continue to wear western attire after her marriage'. Was it such an issue to be stressed upon I wondered. 'And no babies for five years. She must complete her studies.'

'Of course', smiled my husband- to- be. 'She can study and even work should she wish. There's no question of children for the next five years.'

My mother-in-law-to –be looked askance, desiring to express a thought. But was silenced by a brief look from her son. My father, not possessing what I believe to be my womanly instincts missed the exchange. The marriage was finalized.

A month later I was pregnant with my first child. But suffered a miscarriage in the first trimester itself. I had read in a medical journal that by the end of the first trimester, which is about week twelve of pregnancy, the fetus has a recognizable human form. Being a motherless girl I felt increasingly handicapped in dealing with my new state of affairs despite my educated upbringing. (Or was it because of it?) I took a little time breaking into the mould of an acceptable daughter-in-law. Prattling before my father about being mistreated by my sisters-in-law who were so much older than me, I was firmly reproved of failing to live up to his expectations of a responsible daughter. My father's advice was that as a married woman I was no longer to think like a seventeen year old but always behave as the mother of all-even an eighty-year-old if need be. He never tired quoting Kalidas' writing 'On becoming a wife' from the masterpiece Shakuntala, translated to English by A.W.Ryder:

My child, when you have entered your husband's home,

Obey your elders and be very kind

To rivals, never be perversely blind

And with your husband, even though he

Should prove less faithful than a man might be;

Be as courteous to servants as you may,

Not puffed with pride in this your happy day:

Thus does a woman grow into a wife

But self-willed woman are the curse of life.

It was not always easy to mould myself to my father's expectations. At times a little beast inside my heart protested. Sometimes the monster growled like a big demon instigating me to rebel. But I just had to close my eyes and father's trusting visage would appear before me. 'Learn to give, my little one. For there is no greater beauty than a woman giving love, care, understanding—unreservedly.'

His profound words would successfully expose the pettiness of any situation I was making a mountain of. And the problem would miraculously work itself out. For there was never a problem, never a wrong, never a sin. Everything was a creation in my mind. Being infinite I had the power to destroy the negative thoughts creeping dangerously into my disciplined mind. With a simple formula my father had armed me always to be a winner.

Arranged marriages, which are looked upon with so much awe and curiosity by the Western world has a long and enduring track record in India. I was fortunate in that my husband was not a habitual wife-beater or a drunkard or chain smoker. At any age in human history, when the male is without these vices, he is considered to be a good example of his breed. Furthermore, he was very handsome. Most importantly, he belonged to the moneyed background similar to mine. So the nightmarish question of having to adjust to a lower social echelon never rose its ugly head either.

That elusively quintessence tie of love separates all strong bonds from the others. For love to flow our presence needs to be appreciated and that appreciation needs to be reciprocated. Then love doubles. On this premise, many times have I questioned the correctness of my situation.

'Daddy, isn't it wrong to live with a man who doesn't want you in his life *unconditionally*?'

And my father would evade the issue with his didactic viewpoint. 'Can we stop wanting a part of us at any time in our lives? Marriage needs as much hard work as your studies or your profession. The golden rule is that your psyche should always be filled with pleasant thoughts. Be open- minded to forever improve upon even your best when confronted with constructive criticism. Remember, none can trample upon you for you were born to triumph.'

Yes. I triumphed. Like a woman does. Everywhere and always. My father must have left no stone unturned in my upbringing. My husband discovered he could not do without my constant presence in his life. While he had been sizing me up, I had woven and entwined my existence within him without either of us consciously being aware of it.

One day he returned almost stamping his feet and ballooning his face, flinging his files on the floor before throwing himself on the bed. Refusing to voice what the tragedy was. A repetition of this scene made me decide to probe into and settle the matter once and for all. A grudging revelation from the man I had so often trembled to face overwhelmed me. He needed to gaze into my countenance every morning when he left home. The day I didn't walk along with him towards the door wearing a smiling expression, he automatically switched off mentally.

'A wife is the constant and sacred source of life'. My father had once quoted. Was this what he had meant?

Perhaps our lives would have meandered along its journey to eternity had not beauty personified in the body of a woman named Saloni descended upon our lives in all her voluptuous splendour from across the Atlantic Ocean within three years of our marriage. One look at her and for the first time in my life I wished I had been born strikingly beautiful. My husband's unwavering glance from her only heightened that yearning.

She remained with us. She was the daughter of a very dear friend of my father. She was the same age as my husband. She was unmarried. She had been too busy building her career to concentrate on any long-term relationship. Being alone in the city she was entrusted upon us as our responsibility.

I wonder if my father would have been quite so resolute on her staying with us had he actually seen and met Saloni. The last time he had met his friend was during their schooldays when they had studied together in the same school. And from what I could tell from the photographs Saloni carried with her, the pot- bellied curly haired dark man that was her father bore no resemblance to her. It was her mother Saloni needed to thank for bestowing upon her those stunning looks. Rather tall, with a gloriously curved figure, a spotlessly pearl pink complexion and every feature shaped to perfection. My poor husband would have to have been made of rock to remain unaffected by such an alluring sight living in constant close proximity.

It is not that my husband's love for me diminished once Saloni entered our lives. Far from it. In fact, he made an extra effort to shower and demonstrate a great fondness for me publicly even when it went against his very nature. He tried desperately hard to acknowledge and admire all the things in me worthy of appreciation. And when he was at a loss to elaborate upon my limited talents, he even resorted to fabricating and praising me on traits and characteristics I did not in fact possess. *He tried very hard to present me as more than the woman I was in Saloni's presence.* Witnessing his desperation I fervently wished I had a few more skills that he could boast his wife of possessing. Only then did it dawn on me what a favour he had done by marrying me. So typical of his well-meaning nature. Then again, was it necessary to reform oneself to attain appreciation? Won't life be that much simpler and happier if one were to be content with all that one's partner possessed?

Saloni always wore a charming smile in that lovely face of hers. Her eyes sympathized with me. She realized she was blessed in abundance with every attribute my husband so admired in a woman. My husband was aware of it. I knew it.

But we were all caught in this web of love, trust and faith. My husband would never admit that he had actually fallen in love. He had forever ridiculed the concept of being nothing more than a figment of imagination of fools and philosophers. As for Saloni, how could she live with the guilt of stealing away the husband from the woman who had become such a dear friend? In that tangled mess of a triangle I could easily have claimed ignorance of the undercurrents and continued enjoying my position in sublime oblivion.

Life would not have come to a halt. Neither for Saloni nor for my husband and not for me either. Pain would have wretched Saloni's heart. My husband would have concentrated whole-heartedly on burying all those emotions surging within him. I would be the only one unaffected by it all. When Saloni left, I would once again become my husband's sole companion.

Unhappily, I knew I could not live with myself by snatching happiness. Of course I could patiently try to divert my husband's thoughts towards me. He would continue to look after me as he had done before. But it was no longer enough for me. I had glimpsed a yearning portrayed in his eyes when he gazed at Saloni.A look he had failed to control even with his iron –willed determination. Could I carry on enjoying the benefits of being his wife merely because he had married me before love had come to him? Not when I discovered that an endless list of sacrifices, compromises and self-improvement programs were not required for him to fall in love. He had been trying all these years to change me into the woman Saloni already was. Although we did not wish to admit it because it would in a sense mean a colossal failure: we were both tired. Very tired. Trying to be what we were not. Actually.

My father will of course bend his head in grief and shame when he sees me at his doorstep with my bulging suitcase. He may even call me a coward, an idiot with a defeatist attitude .He will illustrate with a hundred examples how marriages have survived bigger, more concrete storms and emerged victorious. He may well call me the female Momus.Like Momus; I too could not fault the perfection of my husband's Adonis body… But I am confident he will one day admit that happiness lies even in bequeathing upon others those who truly do not belong to us. Then he shall definitely admit that I have finally realized the infinite dimension of my name by letting go.

Reality contradicted my hypothesis in condemning my husband of a Pygmalion mindset. My intellect, flush with thoughts gained from the most brilliant minds whose works I have devoured all my life had failed to understand the simple truth that makes a man want to be with a woman every moment of his life. It took me a Saloni to grasp the depth of my husband's devotion. To realize that love is not a butterfly that flutters in gay abandon for a few weeks in springtime. How can an emotion that involves exploration and commitment of two souls ever be underestimated to a temporal triviality?

Needless to say, my husband followed me to my father's house as soon as he discovered I had left home. Looking at his haggard face that appeared to have aged over a decade within those twenty-four long hours I had been away, I realized father was right in his observation that my husband would not know how to continue living happily without me. In the final analysis, it was this felling of oneness culminated over the years that possessed that infinite dimension compared to which all other experiences were but finite acts within it.

VISAGE

It was this appalling appearance, which demanded of everybody to take an instant aversion towards her. From that flushed protruding forehead to the quivering mass of wobbly flesh of a weak chin, the features were all wrong. And it was not simply a facet or an expression that required clever hands to chisel it to an acceptable finish.

Although, people sought her company continually, a foreboding uncertainty troubled her constantly. She became prone to deliberating of her spouse's disenchantment with her even though their marriage could boast of fifteen years of marital bliss. During the early years, the muscles had not sagged quite so much and her countenance had not been quite so alarmingly strange. With age, the skin folded like a pathetic soft sheet of skimmed milk top, deposited carelessly by a finicky old man from the glass of milk and despondently lying in a corner of a plate, shamefully shrinking in the cold, into a myriad tiny wrinkles.

She needed to repair the damage, needed to restore her self-worth before this feeling of inadequacy engulfed and corroded her spirit utterly. After months of self-deliberation, she decided to take action.

All she would disclose to her husband was that she needed a long retreat. That it was vital on reflecting over the significance of her life.

He had initially been apathetic towards her decision of course. Somehow, he wasn't too comfortable with the idea of her taking herself off to some obscure destination with the vague objective of rediscovering her individuality. Why couldn't they go together like they had always done? It wasn't as if he suspected her of any ulterior motive. He trusted her completely. It was just this perplexing sense of uneasiness that had crept into his consciousness, which he with his practical bent of mind failed to decipher.

So he did not stop her. Willing to bear the pain of missing her constant presence by his side. Accepting the painful reality of passing long days merely by hearing her voice over the phone when she choose to call him because she refused to use their cellular phones or give him any contact number. Meanwhile, in the quiet confines of the informally comfortable room of a private clinic, she touched her face with the gentlest fingertips; frightened least the slightest pressure distorted their shape further. She studied for a long moment the familiar face reflected in the mirror and handed herself over to the expert hands of the surgeon whom she had got to know rather well during the course of her sessions with him, the past three months.

It seemed like a long time since she left home. Her husband was growing more frantic by the day, insisting on knowing where she was, desperate to rejoin her. It was getting more and more difficult misleading him about her whereabouts. And she was impatient to see her reflection in the mirror again.

But before permitting her to look at herself again, the doctor took great pains to prepare her for the revelation, emphasizing that he had had to modify the total visage for a flawless creation. He appeared extremely apprehensive of her reaction. His attractively sculptured face twisted with agony. Surely it would be impossible for a skilled professional like him to sully her already wanting image? Why this atypical nervousness from one so competent in his work?

Eventually, when she tentatively glanced at her mirror image however, she was elated. Her facade could now win her back her husband's love. He would love her new face.

Then the problem struck her. It was so perfect because all the original features had been moulded to a new profile, leaving not a vestige of resemblance to the old visage. How would her husband recognize her?

'Why does he need to recognize you?' The plastic surgeon derided. 'Walk into his life as a different person and start afresh.'

The likelihood of being able to pander to her most incredible fantasies sounded too awesome and she gave in to temptation. She wrote a letter to her husband as his wife saying that she was leaving him for good and that he should never try to get in touch with her.

After that, she walked into her husband's life as a brand new acquaintance, introducing herself with a fictitious name when they bumped into each other 'accidentally' at a bar he frequented, a coincidence she had long premeditated upon and meticulously executed. Winning over her reluctant husband's affections was not an exceptionally difficult task to overcome in the vulnerable frame of mind he was in. She utilized her relentlessly persuasive skills to the hilt. It wasn't long before she was enacting the peculiar role of his 'mistress', albeit a very pushy one at that.

In her mind's fanciful vision, their life sailed smoothly as a sailboat in the clear calm blue waters of the sea of her life for a blissfully wonderful period. She could tell her husband was satisfied with her pristine aura. She was beautiful now and her body firm and supple- almost like Aphrodite's rising from the foams of the sea. She was effusive and far more confident than she had ever been before.

Her new *femme fatale* persona filled her with a huge sense of self-gratification. However, she soon discovered a new dimension to her personality she had not noticed before. She feared she was growing a little too possessive of late. She pined agonizingly for her husband throughout the period of his absence every time he left town at the pretext of unexplained official work.

When the little green devil of jealousy that perpetually lurks in the recess of all minds threatened to engulf her in its web of suspicion, she decided to accompany him during one of his official tours and stalked him like a shadow when he left her in their hotel room ostensibly to attend a conference. She failed to fathom as to what more he could want. So any sense of shame she might have felt at spying on him, she justified it as her concern to unravel his undisclosed desire that led him to stray. Suspecting him of infidelity now was absurd especially since he had never cheated on her during the entire period of their marriage.

He was walking so swiftly down the gray, recently rain drenched lane that she had to almost run, dangerously tripping in her red stilettos, to keep him from disappearing out of sight. She saw him enter a tours and travel office. It had glass panels for doors and windows. He entered the bureau and directly went up to the woman who had been intensely engrossed in punching letters in the keyboard of the computer on her table. The woman's profile came directly within her line of vision.

He greeted her with a kiss on her mouth. It was a lover's kiss. She could tell even from such a distance that their lips were familiar to each other. She peered against the mirror and the delicately fashioned tip of her nose flattened against the glass. Her eyes must have started misleading her. How could it be her? *Impossible.* The word kept reeling in her brain. She stood transfixed on the spot as the two of them walked out of the office without even noticing her freezing in the cold dampness, while they were wrapped so snugly against each other, warming the moist air surrounding them with their beguilingly gay laughter.

That night, in their hotel room he recounted excitedly how he had found his lost wife. Elucidating in minute detail why she had left him, thinking she was unworthy of him. How it had taken him so long to convince her finally to believe in his undying love for her. Having at last rediscovered their true love for one another, she had promised to return to him. By agreeing to come back to him she had made him the happiest man on earth.

He left her with a quick peck on her forehead, another apology and, a fat white envelope that contained enough money to last her a lifetime if she used it judiciously. She refused to accept the money declaring it made her feel cheap. He claimed that she had been his dearest friend and would always remain one. He pleaded she keep the money. He wished her happiness and good health and was gone before she could think of a reason to stop him leaving her. How copiously contrite of him! But she couldn't question his conduct in any manner. After all, she had been the one who had aggressively pursued him and taking advantage of his momentary weakness had clung on to him, coiling herself like a muslin sail once rigged against a boat, now careworn by the gale. He had candidly continued pining for his lost wife all the time she had been with him. Considering the circumstances, he had behaved like a gentleman.

The vital point was: *she was here. How could she have been there as well?*

The surgeon had to have an answer. She dialed his number and insisted on a meeting. His home was a splendid chocolate brown villa, a short drive away from the city .The interiors were done up in rich teak wood which exuded a warm and welcoming ambiance.

She got directly to the point. 'What is going on Doctor? Can you explain how I happened to see my old self in a travel agency? How could I be alive like. ...like this? With this new face you have given me when what I was originally born like is still around? *Living. What* have you done to me? Is this some kind of a hypnotic game you are playing? What? Do you have an explanation to what is happening to me?'

'Do please sit down. ' The Doctor urged her quietly indicating to a massive armchair lavishly strewn with floral hand embroidered cushions.

She sat down reluctantly. Her palms tightly pressed together. Her back was stiff and straight. Her graceful long neck delicately bending like a swan, she waited silently.

He paused a long moment before offering an explanation, coughing and clearing his throat before he spoke. 'When I first met my patient I was mesmerized. I had never met anyone half as interesting before and the better I got to know her the more convinced I became that she was the perfect woman for me. I was angry with her husband for not being able to make her secure in his love. I tried my best to dissuade her to forgo plastic surgery and remain just the way she was.'

He confessed brokenly, his husky voice choked with emotion. He had tried the best he could to talk her out of going ahead with the surgery but when she remained adamant, he decided to clone her with the assistance of his best friend who was a genetics professor and sculpt the clone with the finest visage. In this manner, the husband could have his new made- to- order life partner while he could treasure the real woman who would remain untouched by his scalpel. Unfortunately for him, in spite of his best efforts, the wife never learnt to stop loving her spouse and start loving him instead.

He was sorry .So sorry .For everything.

His ramblings made her heart grow cold. 'What do you mean, the real woman? I am real, aren't I? My God, you are not going to tell me that I am a clone! *Am* I?' She asked, her voice thick with tension.

That day, the second man in the life she knew apologized to her. ' Yes. You are the genetic copy I perfected upon. I am sorry.' He said heavily. His shoulders stooped as he hung his head low with a mammoth sense of guilt.

THE SARIWALLAH

He introduced himself as Bhola Nath. A slushy wet mud coloured short stubby, bubbly character in his forties with a bouncing stride that greatly resembled the cantering of an awkward colt. Bhola claimed to be from Dhaka in Bangladesh. Generally, illegal immigrant labourers seeking refuge in India by crossing the over two thousand km-long border, claimed to be Bengalis. The Indo-Bangladesh border in Tripura extends via Dhemagri upto Chittangong Hills on the coast of Bay of Bengal along the Sunderbans to Murshidabad, Jalpaiguri and completes a full circle in Dhubri district. But Bhola Nath who (as I later discovered) actually belonged to *Kolkata* (Calcutta, as I have always known it), claimed to be from Dhaka. It is possible that this small manipulation of facts helped him lend extra authenticity to his business clients.

Every sari speaks about the tradition of the region through its designs. Like the most vibrantly coloured *kancheevaram* from Kanchuipuram, the *patola* with its famous *ikat* technique from Gujarat and Orissa or the colourful *bandani* from Rajasthan and Gujarat.

Showrooms in the neighborhood mall might stock the widest variety of the same product. But nothing compares to this exquisite feeling of self-indulgence in wrapping oneself in yards of cotton or silk purchased from a local where that fabric, famous for its craft, had been woven. For, every Indian woman wants to outwit her peers in her pursuit of that ultimate sari that would drape her body in its folds like a Shakuntala or a Venus.

His target clientele were the sari-wearing women of Assam, Bengal and Orissa. He refused to visit the women of any other region. Perhaps, his comfort level with the women of these regions was more due to his language skills. His Hindi was deplorable. He most certainly did not possess a rich enough vocabulary to persuade prospective customers in any language other than Bengali. As it is, Bengali is a sweet language with a lilting tenor that lends it a poetic cadence. *Jamdani* or the figured muslins are amongst the most exclusive muslins. These muslin masterpieces even had lyrical names like *shabnam* (evening dew), *Malmal khas* (muslin reserved for kings) and *Abrawan* (flowering water) to complement their craftsmanship. In the *Jamdanis* the base is unbleached cotton yarn and the design is woven using bleached cotton yarns to produce a light and dark effect. He could wax eloquent on the *Jamdani* sari with the authority of a well-versed scholar .So it was extremely difficult not to be alluringly awed hearing him speak ex-cathedra on the subject, though he was a businessman whose main purpose in life was to accumulate wealth. Money - that sublime drug that has the power to change a man into a can of greed, not that a woman is any less guilty of all kinds of material extravagances.

As for buying a sari, I didn't have the foggiest idea as to what would suit me best, or what would be the approximate price for any given sari. A friend of mine who sent Bhola across to my house obviously didn't know of my jeopardy. It was a bit awkward to inform her of my absolute lack of knowledge in buying a sari when she rang up to inform me that she was sending Bhola right away. Being a weekday, even my husband who would have proved a great help, was also not at home. The late afternoon being the least busy time of the day, I had no excuse but to agree to my friend's offer. As she put it, this was my hour of luxury. And what better way to pamper myself than to have the pleasure of selecting saris at my leisure in the comfort of my drawing room?

And so entered Bhola Nath with five huge bundles of his exquisite collection packed in coarse white homespun khadi. I can't say what exactly I had been expecting, maybe someone riding a bicycle with a pack of clothes. I had seen small time traders selling their wares thus in tiny towns and villages across India. Most certainly, I was not expecting a merchant with bundles and bundles arriving in a van. He was a short man. And when he bent, as he did ever so often to supplement his eloquence with his body language, I feared his head would hit the floor, causing him injury. He utilized his limbs and facial expressions effusively in persuading his buyer. Without having attended any fancy college for an MBA degree, he proved to be a suave salesman. I did not need a sari at all, yet I found myself being influenced to make a purchase. Interestingly, each sari I chose proved to be more expensive than the previous one. Fortunately, I had flatly refused to even glance at the ones that were in the range of rupees ten thousand and above. He complemented me sincerely on my selection. What great taste I have; I had clearly chosen his very best saris! Not to mention some of the most expensive ones as well. Truly, a lady with a grand taste! He most certainly had the knack of boosting one's ego with the subtleness of a practiced professional. Even a cynic like me secretly felt proud of my own achievement. I must have become a connoisseur in sari selection without even having realized it. Thrilled with myself, I resolved to buy three of his saris.

As I went to the bedroom to fetch the money, Bhola sat down quietly and waited with a satiated look that eased away each worrying wrinkle on his countenance, having convinced and won over his customer.

When I opened my safe, I was in for a shock. I realized to my horror that I did not have enough money to pay his bill. I could barely afford one, let alone three. The thought of not making a purchase after the time and effort he had exhausted made me feel awful. I felt like a cheat who had watched a beautiful play of a great dramatist without paying for the ticket. I went and informed him of my predicament, profusely apologizing at the same time. I offered to buy one. Bhola Nath, ever full of bright ideas, suggested I ring up my husband and ask him to send the money across through a peon. I was most reluctant to follow his suggestion, knowing full well how difficult he could get when it came to spending. More to satisfy Bhola Nath than with any speck of hope, I rang up my husband. As expected, he was livid with me for allowing a Sariwallah within the premises and instructed me to get rid of him immediately. No, there was absolutely no need for me to make any purchases. If I needed any saris he would get them for me. When my husband says something that is the end of the matter. No argument from my side is entertained. Ever.

I looked at Bhola Nath with a remorseful face. I wished I had some money to buy his saris. Apart from the fact that the saris I had selected were stunning, a human rapport tends to build up when someone comes to sell at your doorstep. And Bhola Nath was one of the most amiable characters one could come across. I felt dreadful having to refuse buying his saris. He was a reasonably persuasive sales person. He asked me to look once again if I had money stashed up somewhere. Now that he reminded me, I did have some cash in my purse! Apparently, I now had enough to pay for two of his saris. I felt somewhat absolved of my guilt. I even referred him to a few of my friends who I was sure would buy from him. Those pale brown eyes that constantly wore an earnestly pleading look can tug at a woman's charitable instincts.

Yet he persisted upon my buying the third one as well. By this time my patience was wearing thin. I had made it amply clear to him that I could not afford it. He refused to believe. Now he suggested I take another look at my closet. To humour him I searched every nook and corner of my almirah, ransacking every purse. I showed him the last five hundred rupees that I had salvaged. There was no way I could afford the third sari whose price he had earlier quoted as two thousand rupees. Declaring how eager he was to make a permanent customer, he offered me the sari at that meager price. I presumed he was rather desperate to sell off his saris. As I bade him farewell, a seed of doubt was simultaneously germinating in my mind as to whether I had been fleeced. I quickly brushed aside the niggling suspicion, telling myself that if not for his saris, he certainly deserved a little extra for the dramatic presentation of his merchandise. Complacent at having done my good deed for the day, I put the matter out of my mind.

A week later, one of my friends whom I had referred Bhola to came over in a typically feminine gesture of comparing her purchases with that of mine. Nisha, who generally wears a sari, had purchased seven saris from Bhola Nath. I had implicit faith in Nisha's judgment on saris, her knowledge on the subject being almost encyclopedic. A look and a touch - and Nisha could tell you the precise price of any particular sari. The saris she had purchased were pretty. But when I showed her the ones I had bought, she mischievously teased me on my husband's generosity in allowing me to buy such expensive saris. She held the last one for which I had paid the princely sum of five hundred rupees, lovingly like a priceless piece of jewellery. She remarked, 'I hope you didn't pay more than five thousand rupees for this one. Although, for such an unusual shade I would willingly shell out another couple of hundreds.'

I remained transfixed on my seat. My mind had suddenly become totally blank. I could never ever tell her the exact price I had paid for the sari. I had not paid anywhere close to the amount she had quoted for all the three saris I had purchased.

This strange encounter with the Sariwallah has left me a better person. Now I try not to perceive the entire class of business people with a jaundiced eye and avoid making sweeping judgments about people. Bhola Nath's demonstration of a simple human benevolent trait was probably not in sync with that of his community, proving that greatness in man can be attained through simple actions too.

Passion

He sauntered into our lives as my husband's junior colleague in the finance department. The primary reason for initially inviting him over to our place was to get acquainted with the culture of the state where we had newly been relocated. To my mind, the state of Haryana was unusual and wonderful and a totally novel experience. I had earlier never interacted with anyone from the region. Everything about the area was fascinating and captivating: wide open spaces, rugged Aravalli hills, village women in their petticoat-like *lehangas,* bright blouses and a colourful, brilliantly hued *chunni* covering their head, leaving the midriff seductively exposed; the elephantine buffaloes, the astonishing variety of birds...Songbirds, flycatchers, bulbuls, mynas, sparrows, parakeets, tailorbirds, pigeons, doves and the occasional kingfishers were regular visitors to the area.

Ambling through a nearby village was always a learning experience. A group of elders seated around an ornately decorated *hookah* sat on *charpoys,* discussing topics ranging from the mundane to those of paramount importance in their lives. Their *turbans,* - dyed bright red, orange, brick coloured headgears; lent color to the white *dhoti kurta* they sported. More than the human inhabitants of the village, however, it was in search of the scores of splendid winged creatures that I traversed out into the village. Weaverbirds wove their elaborate, pendant nests in trees short enough for me to stretch out my hand and bring home with me the magnificent booty of their vacated homes they had abandoned to migrate off to a suitable climate. Flamboyant peacocks danced to blatantly show off their train in full plumage perching themselves atop the terraces of every building the eye could meander into. Discarding its historically christened name, I called it the 'village of peacocks'. The village folks treated them with compassion indulging them with millet and broken wheat.

Our new acquaintance, my husband's colleague, Amar Yadav, belonged to the village. It was a prosperous village by any Indian state standard. The houses of the well- to- do were gaily highlighted in olive- green, orange, brick-red as well as all the colours sported by the peacock. Each house had a small room constructed at the landing that housed the staircase. This room with its vividly painted roof resembled a dollhouse from a distance. Every house could boast of a terrace on each floor. The peacocks generally wandered from their habitat in the trees within the village, into the balconies of the villagers' houses condescending to perform an impromptu incredibly elegant dance for the benefit of any awestruck human eye. I could never tire watching them-from every conceivable angle possible. The multitude shades of blue so uniquely their own, mesmerized .The pretty crown with pearl-like protrusions at the tip of the tiara corroborated their status in the looks department.

Our protagonist, Amar Yadav, was a Jat. Joseph Davey Cunningham in his book '*History of the Sikhs*' had spoken highly of them, writing that they formed the 'finest rural population in India' with their willingness to take up arms and to follow the plough with equal vigour. Another interesting fact mentioned was the common saying that if a Jat had fifty rupees, he would rather dig a well or buy a pair of bullocks with the money than spend it on the idle rejoicings of a marriage. Even though the book was first published in 1849 I was amazed at the accuracy of the relevance of the statement even to this day. The Jat was still a hard worker.

Perhaps it was the proximity of his home to ours that fostered the unlikely friendship between my husband and Amar Yadav.Perhaps, it was Yadav's naivety that charmed the urbane city slicker in him. Whatever the reason, an unlikely bond slowly emerged between the two men. I found myself getting more and more curious about Yadav.As a golden unspoken rule; my husband and I do have our select same sex friends with whom we spend time to maintain a healthy breathing space in our relationship. Under normal circumstances we do not encroach upon each other's territory. Yet, as they sat drinking coffee after dinner, discussing Yadav's forthcoming marriage, I was tempted to eavesdrop. Sitting inconspicuously in the corner on a teakwood armchair that had once belonged to my grandfather and which I had stubbornly refused to part with despite my husband's orders, threats and ultimatums, I flipped through timely intervals the pages of the magazine I held in my hands. My ears were fine tuned to pick up the minutest details of their téte-à-téte.

Apparently, Yadav had been in love with a girl for the past seven years. I watched his eyes light up every time he mentioned her name, it was as if the profusion of love he harboured in his heart for her deluged into his eyes. In all my years in this world, I had never seen any man so much in love with a woman -not even in the movies. Except perhaps Rhett Butler's indulgent adoration carved in each crease of his visage. But Rhett had been the creation of a master author, Margaret Mitchell, and the actor had been none other than the very talented Clark Gable. In the final analysis, this romantic hero had been the handiwork of two great creative minds. But this was real life passion unfolding before my inquisitive eyes. When Yadav spoke about Amrita, there was a breathless tremor in his voice; a nerve tickled by the side of his neck, and an uncontrollably foolish grin spread over his intelligent face even as he courteously struggled to maintain a suitably measured smile. A faint tinge of redness stained his cheeks and he flapped his arms nervously as he enlightened my husband on the many excellent character traits of his Amrita. The men in the social circle we moved in were perhaps more accomplished in the sophisticated art of concealing their innermost feelings than this callow young man who let his feelings show.

I watched enthralled as he ceaselessly dwelt upon his endless love for Amrita with child-like candor. He articulated his emotions from the very depth of his soul. Every little movement of his betrayed his passion for her –the intense longing in his voice when he mentioned her, the softening of his facial muscles when he spoke of her, surely with every fiber of his being he worshiped her! Even recounting each little attribute of hers, each great quality of her, elated him. It was rather comical to watch my husband, an athletic fellow with interests in all kinds of sports, try to skillfully maneuver the conversation towards a different theme. But the young man's conversation invariably wandered back to the matters of his heart. His devotion to his love was complete. While this proved an intensely boring topic of conversation for my husband, I listened enraptured. This young man had known his girlfriend for so long, yet all he could think about was being with her every waking moment. Now that he had a suitable job, their marriage date had recently been finalized and he was looking forward to an early pre-monsoon wedding. Although weddings generally took place during the winter season here, Yadav was too eager to wait any longer.

That night, as we retired to bed, my husband could not help sarcastically remark on the irrepressible passions of the youth. I realized we would not be seeing much of Amar Yadav around. He had totally failed to make an impression on my husband.

But I had not banked on Yadav's growing awe and respect for my husband. It had become increasingly difficult for my husband to avoid him as he persistently sought him out. In fact, Yadav began looking up to him as an elder brother and much to my husband's exasperation, probed him on advice relating to matters of the heart. We've been married eighteen years now and my husband and I are definitely done with the initial rush of adrenalin guaranteed to flow when boy meets girl for the first time. With a multitude of interests to keep him busy, my husband always found his patience stretching thin in Yadav's company. It didn't help matters that we were actually conversing about a woman we had not even seen a photograph of. Yadav had been too shy to request her for a photograph (or even click one himself)! So unlike most men who carry a snap of their beloved in their wallets, Yadav did not even possess a photograph of his love.

The ethereal features and persona he attributed to her were hard to imagine in any terrestrial being. If we were to envisage upon his elaboration, she would be a woman so striking that that she would easily put even a beauty queen –in the average looks category. In the absence of photographic evidence, in the event of never having met her, my husband rubbished the very existence of Yadav's love life into a mere fabrication of youthful fantasy run riot. But the lover was an ardent worshipper of his object of desire with a heart flung free of restrictions limited by such mundane matters as facts. I was enchanted hearing him elaborate how he would come as a groom dressed like a prince in a cream colored *achaken*, on a chariot decorated with fragrant, white *rajanigandha* flowers and red roses, drawn by four to eight horses. He even made all the wedding purchases by himself. His enthusiasm was infectious and I found myself eagerly awaiting his forthcoming marriage.

It would have helped finding a most appropriate gift if we had caught even a glimpse of the bride –to – be. Choosing a present for a woman is always a difficult proposition. And if that woman happens to be an unseen lady whose complexion, stature and features you may only meditate upon, the task becomes all the more complex. Finally, I decided to settle for some jewellery, for Yadav appeared most reluctant to show us his prospective bride. Perhaps it was considered inappropriate to introduce one's fiancée to newly acquainted friends.

As the wedding day drew closer, Yadav's feet appeared to be transported from *terra firma* to an extra terrestrial strata and his deep expressive eyes took on an even more dreamy hue with myriad thoughts of his life together with his lady love teasing his senses. He was preparing for his wedding in a frantic frenzy. His family members were left idle, as he single-handedly appeared to handle all the preliminary preparations himself. He was busy purchasing all the garments and ornaments, liaisoning with the tent*wallah*, caterers and the decorators. He had even ordered the buggy drawn by four horses where he would ride up to the wedding venue as the groom. Yadav shyly confided of his plans to take his bride for honeymoon to Kashmir. He even purchased the air tickets and booked a cottage in Pahalgam in Kashmir. It was just a few days wait for the wedding day to approach and to ring in everything gloriously new in our ardent lover's life.

Sadly, that was not to be. Just four days prior to the wedding everything went horribly wrong. Amrita's elder brother who worked in the Gulf returned home with a better proposal for his sister and insisted upon Amrita calling off the wedding.

The precise details of what followed were difficult to come by for Yadav suddenly started avoiding us. He stopped attending office. One day, we decided to pay him a visit. His appearance stunned me. He had lost weight drastically and his eyes had sunk into lost pools of sorrow clouded in a constant film of moisture that he struggled so unsuccessfully to control. As one human being to another my heart went out for the dejected, young man. His normally clean-shaven face was now covered with a messy thick black beard. His shirt was not pressed, though he had always been meticulously fastidious about his dressing. His shabby appearance could not have been a ruder shock.

This was the inevitable pain in passion, I presumed. One could only hope that he would recover and continue with his life. From his incoherent speech, however, it was easy to deduce that he had taken this knock awfully to heart. He was the first man I had met who was willing to die for his love. Offering our condolences and our support-which seemed so trivial considering his monumental loss, we departed.

A few days later we received a call from Yadav inviting us to attend his wedding at the old village temple by the foothills of the Aravalli hills. The ceremony was scheduled at eleven in the morning, the following Monday. He sounded nervous. It was a big gamble he was trying to pull off marrying the girl without the consent of the family. My husband predicted nothing good would come out of this action of his. But I argued that surely Amrita being a qualified chemical engineer had a right to choose her own life partner?

On the day of the wedding a violently destructive storm threatened to suffocate the entire area in a thick coat of sand particles. The wind howled incessantly, precariously bending the brittle tree trunks-dried in the scorching sun, ruthlessly tearing at the glossy, broad, tapering leaves that crowded in spirals at the end of the long branches of the *champa* trees, their weight almost too heavy for the branches to support even during normal times. When the gust of wind finally lulled, we set out to attend Yadav's wedding ceremony. We were already late by half an hour.

As we reached the temple I could see the storm had left its mark on the pristine white marbled grounds of the temple compound. Dry, not yet dead leaves prematurely snatched away from the trees, dirty torn plastic bags and grime and gravel were strewn everywhere. The temple housed a beautiful life- sized statue of *Radha- Krishna* carved in white marble, ornately attired in red organdy material with a lining of glittering gold lace. There were idols of other deities and saints in the smaller temples around the main temple complex but this was the central temple. There were at least forty steep steps that led down to the temple from the vantage point where I stood near the landing of the steps, waiting for my husband to park his car and join me. Another forty steps below the temple led to a pool of water that emptied into a rivulet. Clutching the jewellery box that contained a gold necklace for the bride, I gingerly proceeded to make my way down the steps. Just at that particular moment, the bride and the groom seated by the sacred fire, that had been alighted by the priest for the ceremony, looked up towards my direction and a look of terror swept across their faces. In an instant Yadav was on his feet carrying his petite, fair and lovely bride in his arms and swiftly running down the steps of the temple with the nimble agility of a panther.

Before my dazed sense could even register the situation, an avalanche appeared to have descended where I stood. An elderly man brusquely lifted and planted me out of the line of attack with a curt warning to stay out of the commotion. There were at least a couple of dozen men, all very well-built flaunting wooden sticks in their hands, menacingly charging towards the couple, screaming abuses at Yadav.For a split second, Yadav turned back to assess how fast his enemies were catching up with him. That reflex cost him dear. He missed a step. The young couple rolled down the steep steps like a sack full of potatoes into the water body. Their skulls knocking against the giant black boulder that lay in the middle of the water. Had Yadav not been in such mental turmoil I am sure it would have been a joy walk for him to brave the disturbed waters and escape to safety with his bride. But fate was not in their favour. The waters, which had been crystal clear, were quickly stained red. The posse stood transfixed on the spot, totally appalled by the turn of events. All in a matter of moments it was too late for regrets.

Soon after the incident, my husband was posted to Bangalore and with the years unfolding their many events in our lives, memories of our stay in Haryana regressed to disjointed faded pictures in the mind's gallery.

About ten years later, my husband was again transferred back to the same town in Haryana.Returning to the state evoked the passionate tale of the young local couple to resurface and I was overcome with the desire to visit the temple where the tragedy had occurred. It seemed appropriate that I visit the temple to pay homage to the unfortunate lovers. My husband vehemently refused to go anywhere near the temple. He found even the thought of the incident too morbid to recall.

So one morning, fishing out the jewellery box I had kept with me for ten years, I made my way towards the old temple.

The winter sun was filtering down amidst the deliciously snow white clouds, gently warming the marble portico beneath my bare feet, as I abided by the ancient Hindu custom of walking barefoot in a place of worship. It felt a little foolish, carrying the tan leather oblong shaped jewellery box. I had no clear idea why I had brought it along with me.

The tiny river was no longer present. Human civilization must have dried it out. There was just a small pool of water as a reminder of what had once been a water body. The water was clear with pretty white and silver-gray pebbles sparkling below. There were a few russet coloured pebbles too. I could let my fanciful imagination wander and believe they had been stained scarlet by the blood of the lovers.

A priest, draped in a yellow cotton stole approached me extending his services should I wish to make an offering to the deities housed there and offer my prayers. I consented. He insisted on showing me around the entire temple complex, which housed at least half a dozen small temples dedicated to a particular god or a saint. Finally, he ushered me to a temple situated to the left at the end of the passage of the last forty steps that emptied into the pond. There was a tiny passage that led into a dark cave. At the entrance of the cave was placed the statue of a couple delicately carved out in marble. An earthen *diya* was lit even at this hour. The good priest informed that this small temple was built in the memory of a young couple who had sacrificed their lives for their love at this very spot. A few probing questions on my part established the fact that this nook had indeed been sanctified in the memory of the young lovers-Amar and Amrita Yadav.

I requested the priest to get me a tray of *diyas* filled with pure *ghee* and a packet of incense sticks. I lit the *diyas* and the *agarbattis* and placed the brightly lit tray on the shaded, cold, marble slab. Taking out the necklace I requested the priest to adorn the image of the young girl with the ornament. He carried out my request. Pure lustrous gold sparkled spiritedly, its warmth almost vitalizing life into the wanly beautiful Amrita.

What would Yadav be whispering now? Perhaps:

'I Love thee with the breath, smiles, tears, of all my life! -And if God choose, I shall but love thee better after death.'

The Taxiwallah

I am not sure the term 'taxi driver' aptly describes the effervescent character of Kishan Lal Kumar's profession. Kishan Lal is the owner of the three vehicles he drives as his taxis. He owns a medium sized car for middle class clients, a SUV to accommodate the business class and a luxury sedan to cater to the needs of his higher end patrons. He does not trust others to drive his cars. Therefore, he has not employed any drivers and only one of his cars is available for hire at a given time. I loathe driving, which makes me a strange species amongst contemporary women, one probably as extinct as the dinosaur. So when I can afford to splurge in the luxury of a hassle free ride in a taxi I often hire his mid sized car for my visits to Delhi.

The drive from the outskirts of Delhi where I reside, to my workplace takes almost an hour and the few minutes when I am not busy answering or making calls in my mobile, I converse with Kishan Lal. Whenever I pose a question, his face lights up. He's probably used to endless conversation. I can see words bubbling within him when I am in a position to give him a little attention. In all probability, I am his least communicative passenger. I travel to my office where I generally spend around four hours. After that I proceed to the club for lunch with my friend and then return home. I give him extra money for lunch which he accepts with a wide grin and acknowledges, 'Thank you for the present.' For him it is economical viability versus boredom, I guess. All that waiting cannot always be easy.

Like I said, when I am not too preoccupied, I talk. He lets out a sigh of relief when I pose a question or make a passing comment on such inane topics as to the condition of the world .One word. One sentence. That is all it takes to free the floodgates of his verbal deluge. I encourage him to speak. Apart from the fact that he is an extremely undemanding conversationalist, (I rarely need to interject a response to his monologues), he happens to possess a wealth of information on all local issues. Thus, apart from the advantage of a comfortable ride, I get a free insight into the local culture, traditions, politics and neighbourhood gossip.

During a cold winter evening, I was returning in Kishan Lal's car after presenting a paper at a seminar in the University. The singularly short winters can be bitterly harsh even in the hot landmass of northern India such as Delhi and its neighboring areas. The seminar had been a memorably enriching experience .It was one of life's rare, most precious moments, when one is at peace with all that life offered one. Without consciously realizing what I was doing, I hummed a joyful tune as the car purposefully ate the miles.

'Madam is in a good mood today', observed Kishan Lal, desperately seeking a cue to start a conversation.

'Yes, Kishan Lal.The day has been a fruitful venture. The points I made relating to caste and gender equality were well received by the intellectuals. I am happy because they have agreed to take up the issues I put forward in my paper in a prestigious forthcoming volume on the subject.' I smiled complacently.

'It must be nice to talk about such burning issues and have so many scholars hear what you have to say and debate on the proposals.' Kishan Lal remarked. 'But does anything concrete actually get done for the betterment of the ignored society? Is, say a Dalit, really as free as the upper caste Indian?'

I had never seen the jovial Kishan Lal so serious. It had not crossed my mind that Kishan Lal may perhaps be a so-called 'low caste'. I was unaware of the sense of alienation a person could feel in a modern democracy simply because of his caste. I was far more ignorant than I had ever realized. From Kishan Lal's heartfelt tone it was obvious that he had at some point in his life personally experienced discrimination. I had recently read with avid interest about the sandstone Lakshminarayan temple in Wardha, built by a wealthy cotton merchant, which opened its doors to people of all castes in 1928, ignoring the rigid caste structure.

Unfortunately, for every educated person who endeavours to broaden the human perspective, there are a hundred literate dogmatic fundamentalists who try to retrace the forward march of a humanitarian feat by regressive measures.

'I am sorry Kishan Lal .Has there been any incident you wish to share with me?' I queried as gently as I could so as not to hurt his previously bruised self-esteem.

Kishan Lal abruptly brought the car to a standstill by the side of the road. Before I could reprove him for his hasty action, my glance was arrested by the sight of hail stone sized drops of tears rolling down the high cheekbones of his bronzed rugged face. The sight of a six-foot tall fifty-year-old man crying, momentarily perplexed me until the humane chord that binds us all human beings as an entity surfaced and I found myself patiently waiting for him to speak.

'Can we ever hope to be liberated of upper caste dominion in this free country of ours? Will we ever be free to go anywhere we desire within the country without attracting a negative response? Can we visit all public places without people sneering at us? Forget our generation, can we even hope that our children will ever feel equal? For all understanding, we are dirty and unacceptable in person and surroundings.

'Hari was a meritorious student.'Kishan Lal continued with a distinctive note of pride in his voice. ' He qualified for the engineering seat in the general quota. He was so elated at being a part of the unreserved category. He must have nurtured a hope of becoming one of them by being at par with them.

'But even during admissions some of the professors unnecessarily harassed him. We had no one of our caste working or studying at the institute with whom Hari could have a discussion with while sharing a cup of tea. You understand, to dissuade his fears, comfort him when any issue upset him. Guide him. After all, he was just a teenager, not yet fully equipped to deal with all the ills of the world. He was a state level athlete. He was God's gift to me .The very best child a father could ask for in this world. He filled our lives with laughter. Simply looking at his face I felt I had attained my nirvana.'

Kishan Lal choked as he spoke. 'It's three years since he left us. We were told that he committed suicide. Within six months of his joining the institute. Our son whom we loved more than life itself and who always spoke to me of his ambitions of buying a house for the family in the posh colony where our caste could not be instantly identified. Of taking us all to a foreign place for a holiday like the big sahibs do.'

'Why?' I wondered. Why would a young man pursuing an engineering course in a prestigious institute belonging to a stable family suddenly take his life? I must have thought aloud for Kishan Lal answered.

'He was disturbed by the degrading caste innuendoes some of his peers consistently subjected him to. He was not physically assaulted, you understand. Not even verbally abused directly. So no punishable offence was committed against him. He was simply consistently made to *feel* inferior. Those boys destroyed Hari's self esteem. The atmosphere must have affected him more than I could ever comprehend for it forced my brave son to destroy the life he had so taken care of when he was at home with us.'Kishan Lal sniffed brokenly, rubbing his tear stained cheeks with the back of his hands like a little boy.

'If I had had even an inkling of the extent to which the new society was affecting him I would never have let him go. There was no need. No dire necessity for social prestige. For acceptance into the societal mainstream where so few members of our caste are so grudgingly admitted into. What does it matter that the upper castes choose not to eat and drink with us? Why is their acceptance so important for our fragile egos? Even I shrink every time a upper caste looks at me disparagingly and indistinctly mutters '*sala*' .It takes my wife a whole evening to make me get out of my black mood.'Kishan Lal said.

'It really shouldn't matter, what other people think. What is important is to continue living and striving towards your own perfection'. I mouthed my convictions a little hesitatingly.

'Only if we were allowed, Madame. Only if we were allowed.'Kishan Lal spoke in a melancholy tone. 'It is not possible to live in a segregated world of our own within the society. We need to interact if we wish to progress. But interaction with us is frowned upon. Madam, we cannot go and pray at the temple of our choice without there being a hue and cry over it. Our women are not allowed to draw water from that of an upper caste village well. Their children do not invite our children to their birthday parties and offer them a slice of birthday cake in the same fancy plates they offer them to the other children.

'Tell me, will our students ever experience the confidence of having at least one teacher to confide in if the necessity arose? Madam, when I see the people around me talk so big about progress and modernization I forget that their hearts are still as small as a dry wrinkled pea. Once, just a year back, my wife offered tea to the Madam I worked for earlier, when she visited our house the day after I failed to turn up for duty due to ill health. Do you know what she said?'

'What?' I asked.

'She said (and I quote her exact words):

"You vermin .I employ you giving you a chance for a good life and look how you repay me. Your whole caste deserves to rot and die. How can you shirk your responsibilities so callously? You could have informed me yesterday that you would be absent today. You make me walk into your low caste colony and your wife has the cheek to offer me tea. How dare you take advantage of the goodness of my heart? Doesn't your wife know I cannot and would not accept even water from those of your caste even if I were dying of thirst? Doesn't she have that much sense?" Her voice rose to a crescendo as she vented her anger.

'It was useless trying to explain to her that I had fractured my leg late the previous night while returning from the vegetable market with two sacks full of fresh vegetables. There are no streetlights in our lanes and my leg slipped into the newly dug drain near my home. My neighbours took me to the hospital and my leg was cast in a plaster. My wife did not know the way to the Madam's house. There was no one else in the house. None of the neighbours were free to run errands for me. Tell me how could I have informed her? I could not even ring her up because there was no PCO booth close by.

After I was dismissed from her service the first thing I did once I recovered was purchase this cell phone.' He proudly flashed a bright red coloured cell phone.

'This phone has brought me luck .The day after I procured this phone my sister arrived with a copy of my uncle's will wherein he had left a lot of property in my name. You see, my uncle had no sons and had always looked upon me as his own .The land would not have amounted to much a couple of years back, when he made the will sometime before his demise. My uncle had given my sister the will for safekeeping but you know how women are. No offence to Madam. But being illiterate, she presumed it was merely a worthless stamped letter. Luckily, with the sudden skyrocketing of property prices in all our villages in the vicinity of the national capital, I was able to sell off my inheritance at an astronomical amount. I purchased my cars with some of the money. Now look at me .I am a rich man.' Kishan Lal paused in his long-winded speech with a flourish.

'Yes. But tell me what happened to your son.' I prompted him to retrace his memory to the subject of our discussion.

'Hah, Hari was forced to die.'Kishan Lal declared assertively.

' But I thought you said that he committed suicide.' I asked.

'They left him no alternative.' He declared. 'They made his life impossible. Poor Hari. My Poor Hari.'Kishan Lal spoke disparagingly. Again I saw tears roll down his cheeks. His swift change of emotions rather amazed me. It takes great provocation for me to lose my cool and once I lose my temper it takes me even longer to regain my composure. But Kishan Lal was capable of changing his emotions as quickly as a seasoned theatre artist. Only, his feelings were real, his pain genuine, his tragedy irreversible-for this was no enactment of a scene in a play.

'If you had any inkling of what was happening to him why didn't you make an attempt to help him?' I asked.

'One only becomes enlightened after analyzing the occurrence of an incident. Hari never let me know he was facing any problems, which he could not handle. He would never dream of causing me anxiety. He always wanted to protect us. Always. But they did not let him live.' Kishan Lal concluded.

'They?' I queried.

'The other students. They made him feel like a parasite. That is what he wrote in his letter. A bloodsucking parasite. My son. Whom we had brought up with all our love and hope was called names. Hari had not stolen anything that belonged to them. He had always extended his help to anyone who needed him. In his letter he wrote he hated being born into his caste. He wrote he would never be able to erase this fact from his being. That it would always act as a deterrent to every action in his life.' At this point, Kishan Lal appeared to gulp air as if to fill his lungs with oxygen.

'He had always confided in me before he joined the engineering college. But once he went to hostel he became quiet. I thought it was a part of the growing up process, you know. Had he given me even a hint of the depth of his despair, I would never have let him remain in the hostel. He was more precious to me than any achievement or service he could have qualified for. Hah, the sly games these sophisticated young ones have learnt to play from their parents. How could our innocent Hari have become skilled in taking at his stride his cunning urbane counterparts' malicious remarks? You can see us, we are simple folks with no idea about the complexities of the world beyond our village.' He fished out a passport sized coloured photograph wrapped in a plastic cover, from his ill fitting blazer pocket and trust it into my hand.

'Look at him. This is what Hari looked like. Tell me if he isn't the most handsome young man you have seen!'

I scrutinized the photograph in my hand. It was the photograph of a young man around nineteen. He looked every bit like a rich man's son with fair plump cheeks not yet chiseled with the harsh experiences of maturity. He had obviously been well protected from the ravages of the world outside by his doting parents. Despite his rotund appearance his eyes arrested my attention. In direct antithesis to his well-fed appearance, he had the sensitive eyes of a hungry artist-eager to learn about life in its wider perspective-beyond the realm of petty constrictions .He had the dreamy eyes of a thinker. I knew instinctively he would have made a difference to the world had he lived long enough .How could a person who had such a depth of understanding in his eyes be so fatalistically dissuaded from his mission in his life? They did not appear to be the eyes of a loser but those of a person who was capable of winning against all odds.

Just goes on to show how wrong life can go at times. *A momentary lapse of control is probably all it took for Hari to end it all. Forever.* It must have been harder on him to tolerate discrimination than it had been for his father. After all, Kishan Lal never went to school, never learned that all human beings were born equal, never viewed the whole world as being based on the Atman.... Kishan Lal probably did not know enough to hurt as much.

From Kishan Lal's dialogue I understood that in our country, caste system is the most powerful seminal system. It is not merely hierarchical but authoritarian as well. It is still the caste system, which decides who studies where, who rules, who gets the job, who gets the promotion. Our caste-obsessed society demands an appearance of our agreement even when we are not willing to comply, forcing acquiesce by the sheer weight of political and economic dominance. Meditating upon the subject it appeared to me all the hullabaloo about reservation will mount to nothing unless people of all castes learn to develop a broad outlook on life. For the world to see, India is looking good. But our thoughts are still frozen in the bygone era.

I could not help contemplating this horrific incident may perhaps have been averted if Hari had met someone to confide in at the institute. Someone who would have sympathized with his bewildered state of mind without ridiculing his apprehensions. Like his father said, someone he could share a cup of tea with and articulate his worries. Someone who treated him as a social equal, someone who assessed the true meaning of education as being an instrument of human progress and did not exploit it as a weapon of destruction of unity. I am not asserting it would have been *the* solution. But it might have helped prevent a valuable life. Like Kishan Lal mentioned, no caste, no race, no ethnic group can live in splendid isolation in this modern world.

Kishan Lal may not have attended any school or read a single book in his entire life but he possessed the basic wisdom of survival: that of accepting every challenge every day as an integral part of living and being grateful for anything one obtains without any hard work as a blessing.

As Kishan Lal started the vehicle and purposefully drove me back home, I remember fervently wishing his son had divined this most valuable lesson in life from his intelligent father.

Bribe

The preliminary examination was a difficult experience,the effort to concentrate,to constantly rein her thoughts from wandering away to her brand new handsome husband required immense will-power. Within a week of her wedding she had found herself taking the examination to fulfill her father's long-standing aspiration of her becoming an officer. Even Aroop gently prodded her to attempt the tests.

But this examination which qualified her for the final assessment was an unnecessary bother. If Aroop so much as hinted that she give the tests a miss she would have avoided them in a trice. The results were declared at a time when she was heavily eight months pregnant. The idea of appearing in front of all the other candidates with her figure resembling that of a malnourished child-with an enlarged belly awkwardly protruding out of her dangling limbs was abominably unappealing. But the realization that an additional salary was essential to meet the household expenses, particularly with the arrival of a new member, became agonizingly clear to her.

Attempting the three-hour long papers were more of an ordeal than she had ever imagined. The sniggering of fellow candidates as they stared at her waddle her way into the examination hall with her very pregnant body was the least of her list of awkward discomforts she had to endure. Her body, which she had taken so much for granted all her life suddenly refused to bid to even her smallest command. The sheets of blank white paper stared at her inviting her to pen down every answer she knew so well, urging her to stretch the limits of her physical endurance. But the bile rushing up her throat refused to be suppressed as she barely managed to excuse herself from the examination hall and rush to the toilet.

When she returned to the examination hall a quarter of an hour later, her sickness had not subsided. Her baby was hungry. It kicked robustly. She feared her delicate stretched skin would tear to expose him to the world that very moment. (How did she know her baby would be a boy? Perhaps, a mother's intuition? She simply knew). She tried soothing him by gently stroking her belly beneath the folds of her sari. But another spasm of nausea wrecked her body. She abandoned the three-hour paper within half that time. As she walked to the car Aroop expressed his displeasure with a deafeningly vocal silence.

Her slender limbs had swollen up to unshapely lumps of flesh by the time she reached home. She went and rested quietly on her bed. Defeated and alone. Her failure was a forgone conclusion. No one spoke to her. She had shattered too many hopes. She wept alone with frightful thoughts strangling her survival instinct.

Her baby had been due three weeks later. But the next day when she visited her gynecologist she was admitted to the hospital immediately and the baby was born the following day. A beautiful bundle of life as fresh as a tightly closed pink bud, ready to gently burst into life. This was her life now. A home. A husband. A son. A family. She was happy. If only her in- laws didn't keep persisting that she work. But then ever increasing expenses had to be met. Maya promised her mother-in-law she would start applying for a suitable position as soon as her son was a year old.

However, fate appeared to have other surprises in store for her. The interview call letter arrived just as her son turned two weeks old. It was as if the Gods above had blessed her. She had harboured no hope of ever clearing the main examinations. She had been medically in a most unfit position to take the exam. But some powers above were surely blessing her. Otherwise could she have qualified for the interview?

The call letter changed her life. Her mother-in-law was no longer cross with her over trivial issues. Aroop was so much more amiable. It was almost possible to imagine that he loved her again. Lack of finances would no longer dangle its ugly head ominously like the hangman's loop. With her salaried position, the family would be assured of a comfortable existence. On the day of the interview Aroop considerately took her to the office in his car insisting on waiting for her. She fervently prayed that she successfully clear the interview. If she qualified for the post she would make Aroop happy and in his happiness lay hers. Economic independence may be a modern concept but the need to be loved is surely as old as humanity itself.

Her interview, which had been confirmed for eleven a.m. was rescheduled for two p.m. Maya panicked. The drive to the office had taken over an hour. Her breasts were already beginning to hurt. Swollen hard with excess milk. Arnav must be crying of hunger by now. He had been sleeping when she left home. He was a hungry little one, who, when awake, needed to be fed every forty-five minutes.

Her *muga pat* (silk) *mekhla chaddar* coiled around her sweat drenched body in the humid July heat as the creaking white fan, a remnant of the British era groaned from its elongated rod in a lethargic effort to chase the heat of the day. When her name was finally announced to proceed to the interview room, an immense sigh of relief escaped her. At least the ordeal would be soon over. She knew the interview was strictly speaking, a formality. Her cousin who had faced the interview board the previous day had informed her that she was asked merely a couple of general questions-where did she live? How did she plan to manage working once she married?

Maya walked into the room where two distinguished looking senior officers sat across an impressive conference table. She was conscious of the swish swash noise her silk *mekhla* made in the friction against her sweat laden cotton petticoat clinging heavily to her legs restricting the simple act of walking to an awkward pantomime. (Why had she let her mother get her way in persuading her to wear a silk *mekhla chador* instead of a light cotton one?) The senior interviewer stared at her in stone-faced reproving silence making her even more squeamish. The other board member, however, appeared kinder. Offering an encouraging smile, even praising her precise answers.

But the senior member, the Chairman, was irritated by her lack of ability to respond rapidly to the volley of questions he fired at her. Maya knew even before she closed the door and walked out of the room that her chances of clearing the interview were negligible. The Chairman had brusquely dismissed her answers even before she could complete answering them.

They later learnt that the interview was a farce. The faith of the candidates had been decided prior to their appearing for the interview. The Chairman had signed the offers of appointment of the successful candidates even before the interview was conducted. Rumour had it that each selected candidate had given a sizeable sum of money on the sly to the Chairman for a post while Maya had sat on her high horse of ideals and integrity. This peccadillo on the part of the Chairman left a scar in Maya's life. A permanent taste of ash- of burnt hopes and dreams pervaded her mouth as a reminder of her failure.

Returning home, tragedy struck with pitiless persistence. Her baby, who would have offered her boundless comfort in her hour of need, was snatched away from her as well. A tiny bit of coconut from the *prasad* offered to the Gods above, entreating their blessings for Maya's success had choked him. An Aunt had lovingly fed the morsel to the little one. The doctors were unable to save the baby who arrived at the hospital much too late—delayed needlessly due to the hysterical commotion of the well-meaning relatives. Without a warning. Without suffering any illness. As if the Gods were bent on testing the limits of her endurance.

Her husband attempted to help her regain her faith in herself. Tried to urge her to get her life back in order. But for months she refused to let go her pain and start afresh. How long could he continue being understanding to her uncommunicative stance and carry on trying to quiet his mother's incessant nagging for a grandchild? In a fit of madness he speeded down a hill and his body was cremated in the flames of his favourite car. This was his one and final act of defiance against his mother.

Maya's life fast-forwarded from that of a carefree young woman to a mature woman within those couple of years. The rose hued glasses she had looked upon the world with were discarded as the gossamer sheet of lifelong security of marriage ripped apart to reveal the eternal loneliness of a human being.In a world where living had seemed reasonably comfortable, security collapsed overnight into nothingness. Her mother suffered massive attacks of depression and raved and ranted every time she came face to face with Maya. Her poor father, ever sensitive to his wife's moods, failed to find the correct words to entreat Maya to remain away from her mother. It was left to Maya to gracefully make her exit and avoid needlessly exacerbate the situation. It wasn't the easiest thing in the world for a woman without possessing professional qualifications to search for a 'respectable' position in a competitive market. Another attempt at any of the competitive exams for any Company was economically not viable. Fortunately, her childhood passion for photography helped her secure lucrative assignments as a photojournalist. And within a period of two short years she was able to afford her own little flat and a second-hand car.

Her economic independence was the cachet that enhanced her position in her mother's eyes. Perhaps it was just that her mother didn't feel quite so desperate anymore when she saw Maya capable of standing on her feet. Maya experienced a huge weight off her mind when she noticed the numerous worry lines etched so deeply in her mother's countenance ease a little. Gradually, it was accepted that Maya could live a good life even without a husband. She was involved in her work and rarely managed to make time to go and meet her parents. Her work offered her fulfillment.

What had started as a small means of somehow eking out a livelihood consumed her mind and soul. And the passion she experienced in her work, the pleasure she derived from it surpassed any significant emotions she had ever known save the unbounded elation she had felt at the birth of her child. Arnav had come to her life like the dazzling rays of the early morning sun and left her just as swiftly with lingering memories of his laughter and presence for her to seek solace in moments of deep dejection.

She had a lot to be grateful for. Her work had not only elevated her financial position but brought her a considerable amount of fame as well. The present swept in a new meaning to her life. The past, however, has a tendency of poking its ugly head up when one no longer desires to remember. It happened one night. She had just cuddled in her bed with a hot meal of Chinese takeaway and switched on the television when the doorbell rang. Her mother and father were at the door. But they were not alone. A couple accompanied them. The lady was an old friend of Maya's mother. However, it was the first time Maya was meeting her. Without ceremony, her mother in her blunt manner let her know that Bora Uncle and Aunty needed fifteen thousand rupees urgently as a loan. She would be doing a good deed by lending the money. To her mother, Maya needed to be a paragon on social conduct. They required the money as their contribution toward Mr. S.K. Das, their daughter Devika's, father-in law's funeral. The same Mr. S.K. Das who had interviewed her all those years ago. The Chairman who had so ruthlessly eliminated her in the interview and destroyed every dream she had nurtured even before they could sprout and grow; whose action had cascaded in leaving her a motherless widow. In the early years after her baby's demise she had contemplated a thousand different deaths for Mr. Das. Prayed every time she looked at her son's photograph that some day she would be in a position to disgrace the man whose high position society had acknowledged.

And now, here they were. His daughter- in- law, Devika's parents. Requesting financial assistance from her—a virtual stranger. True, they were acquainted to her parents. But that barely justified their presence in her home at this late hour requesting a loan to save their family honour and prestige.

Maya looked at the aged couple sitting on her drawing room sofa. So humble now that the monetary scale had tilted in her favour, entreating her to lend them money for none other purpose but to be used for the last rites of a man whom she wished to erase from her memory as well. Looking at the flickering emotions of hope, uneasiness and uncertainty dominate their expressions; Maya knew she was incapable of revenge. She couldn't let this old couple stoop much lower. She realised that Devika's parents would forget her generous gesture as soon as they walked out of her door with the money. She was also painfully aware that having recently invested in a new car ,lending money would place her in a financially difficult situation that month.

Yet, she signed the cheque, understanding they were merely parents entreating even a stranger's help for the benefit of their child. Maya watched their relief written large over their withered faces. Their daughter would be spared the ignominy of ever hearing a snide remark from any member of her family about her parent's inability to make a small contribution towards the funeral expenses. It could of course well be a non-issue in her in-law's family. But her parents would never want her to ever feel that they had in any way failed her while fulfilling their duties. The aged couple left along with her parents after a ceremonial show of gratefulness. No elaborate expression of gratitude as a gesture to ameliorate their relation with Maya was thinkable. Not while having to accept money from a woman whose status was so down the social hierarchy. Maya accepted this stark verity .Yet thanked the gods above for their blessings. Always.

Swimming Pool

Circa 2005.A time of rapid social change in India. A superficial urbanization of society with metros, cities, towns and villages influenced by the twentyfour hour cable television beaming on your face a hedonistic lifestyle. Money was no longer a commodity to be stored away in the vaults and lockers. Flaunting wealth was the new mantra of the young and the old alike. No longer was the middle-aged willing to mature gracefully, the senior age group was still groping to come to terms with their advancing years. Trying to steal, hide, and wish away their age with endless sessions of beauty treatment, plastic surgery, botox shots, yoga, ayurvedic treatment, et all—people desperately wanted to believe that they could remain young forever.

Age, which had never been in fashion in any period in history, was never before so old fashioned a concept as it was now. Happily, men even close to one's father's age resented being addressed as 'Uncle' (a very modern trend, I must acknowledge). But it was still perfectly permissible for his unmarried daughter same age as a married woman to address the latter as 'Aunty' (pseudo-modernism?) This was claimed giving due respect to one's marital status.

Initially suburbia life tantalized with Italian marbled floors, American kitchens, European styled country homes and wedding cake- like finish of the spanking new apartments; with swanky malls all brightly lit with larger than life size hoardings of semi –clad models showing off their well toned, digitally morphed bodies; with super-sized luxury sedans dominating the motorway. And swimming pools in every locality.

Living in a neighbourhood during its nascent stage of growth, the advent of anything new is never heralded with great fanfare. There is always something novel. Different.Therefore always exhilarating. But the enthusiasm one fine day amongst the ladies in the colony was almost tangible. The air was heavy with anticipation.

It was the formal inauguration of the swimming pool in the colony that put the ladies in a tizzy. They were mostly housewives who had dedicated their married lives to the upbringing of their children and to devotedly fulfilling all the duties expected of a good Indian wife. As schoolgirls, they had rarely mastered the courage to plunge into the swimming pool in the small towns and cities they generally came from. The swinging seventies saw only the so-called 'hip' crowd indulge in such extravagant activities as swimming and dancing. The eightics and nineties at least had those pools included in the sports complexes to downgrade swimming to less of an elitist sport. But it was only now, with the turn of the century that the sanctity of swimming pools being the exclusive indulgence of the upper class was broken with pools being constructed almost as a mandatory requirement in the middle class housing colonies in the suburbia. With the cable flashing a zillion advertisements on beauty care products for a fairer complexion and innumerable ways to enhance one's appearance, the presence of the swimming pool made it an immediate necessity to work hard on improving the unsightly patches of neglected skin and cellulite thus far unexposed from general view.

Thus we had Mrs. Gupta and Mrs. Sharma sweating it out in the afternoons instead of seeking respite in their siesta.

The gym no longer remained the domain of the muscleman and the obese but the pivotal place for the ladies to trim and tone their shapes to as close to perfection as possible .The hitherto self indulgent wives resisted the temptation to gratify their hunger for the calorie laden *mithais* and *namkeens*. Rich *Kanchipuram* silks, starched cotton *Dakhai* muslins, were quickly abandoned for short *kurtis* paired with a pair of jeans or an ankle length crinkled skirt.

Fusion was 'in'. Fusion (Indo-Western) dressing. Fusion movies, music, language (Hinglish). Fusion décor. Fusion food. Although the traditionally used mustard oil was still a comparatively cheaper and equally healthy cooking medium, Mrs. Gupta wasted no time in substituting cholesterol laden *vanaspati ghee* with branded Italian olive oil as a healthier alternative to cooking Indian meals.

Burmese rubies, Chinese emeralds, Australian Opals, African Diamonds-Mr. Gupta gifted her with precious pieces of jewellery from every corner of the world he traveled to- while participating in the numerous official conferences. It didn't worry Mrs. Gupta any longer-Mr. Gupta's indiscreet liaison with his voluptuous secretary. After the children had left the nest and the husband started spending more time abroad once he climbed the senior level up the corporate ladder, Mrs.Gupta found herself at a crossroad. There was no one left in the house to cook all those dishes she had learnt in her home science classes and in Mrs. Taneja's famous bakery classes. The children's visits were infrequent. And Mr. Gupta, with all his restrictions of maintaining a good physique rarely indulged in a rich cooked meal. Mrs. Gupta had never been a bright student. She had no illusions about her plain looks. But she was immensely proud of her achievements. She had played badminton in school. She had been a fine wife and an obedient daughter-in-law. She had been a dedicated mother. Now she was at a loss.

Time hung suspended as days dragged in her suburbia villa while she waited for the bell to ring .For someone to come to chase away her loneliness-if only for a few hours. Then she would reminisce endlessly about her visits to her children's homes to her colony friends-wives of officers, several belonging to her own age group, many her juniors, very few her seniors. She needed material to sustain her conversation with her friends. How many days could she wield on about her grandson's admission into the best school or about her granddaughter winning all those prizes for elocution. Moreover, she found that she could not master all that zeal her mother had so effortlessly enthused on her grandchildren's achievements. Quite frankly, she was not really interested in harping endlessly about their achievements to the ladies who were even less interested in listening. She was proud of the accomplishments of her children and grandchildren. But their lives could not be the sole reason for her existence.

The swimming pool was just what had been lacking so far in her life to make it that little bit more exciting. Her collection of six swimsuits –all in shades of scarlet miraculously rejuvenated her. The swimming pool added a fresh dimension to her life; it gave her an opportunity to learn something new; to enjoy the freedom of a physical activity. Her newborn self-assurance made her view the world from a more positive perspective. She became involved in her own progress after all those years of being involved in everyone else but herself. *Life was no longer a monotonous waiting room for visitors to come and go*. Her life was happening! At last!

Lifestyle changes always carry with them the burden of adapting to the new from the much threaded upon path. The older one ages the more inconvenient it obviously becomes to let go of creature comforts and quirky habits. But there is no age to restrict self-indulgence. And our ladies, most of them well into their forties and fifties sought to don the swimsuit in their avatar as sexy sirens, an intrinsically womanly desire. One would have assumed Mrs. Gupta, was past the girlie games of looking pretty and giggling. That she was well into the mould of a doting grandmother. Happily,no such senile thought had ever crossed her mind. It was easy to observe that she was relishing life with her afternoon Kitty parties in the company of her bosom friends, all bejeweled and bedecked in the most expensive diamonds and clinging chiffon saris. Gold was oh so old fashioned and those silks and starched cottons did nothing to show off a well-toned figure.

They discussed about themselves lounging at the poolside. Compared notes on how many inches they had lost from their waistlines during their last workout at the fitness center; about how time now did not quite stand still as it had earlier when they were left to content themselves with age appropriate activities. They still enjoyed their Kitties and their *satsangs*. But nothing compared to the *fun* they had at the pool.

The cherry on the icing to her story was when Mrs.Gupta found that she could artlessly respond to Mrs.Baruah's 'Hullo'. That slim and trim Anita Baruah, the wife of the General Manager who sinuously glided like a snake in the pool. Her brand new belief in herself gave her the confidence to return Mrs. Baruah's greetings. And she discovered that she did not hate Anita quite so much once they started exchanging notes on classical cinema- a subject in which they both shared a common interest. Thus remaining true to nature, Mrs. Gupta no longer felt old.